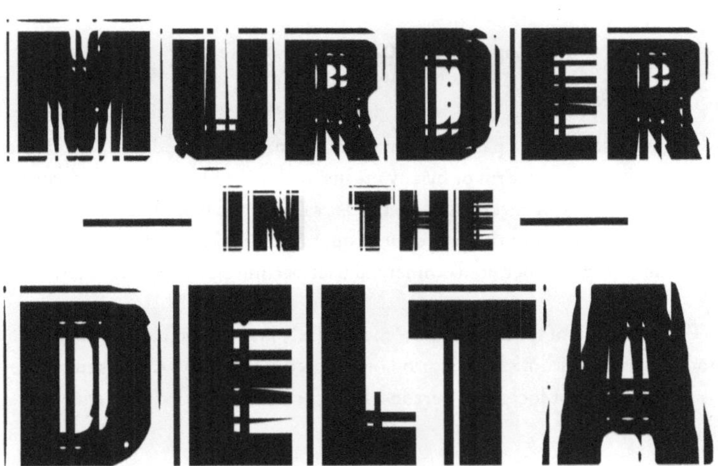

MURDER IN THE DELTA

BELINDA STEVENS

Copyright © 2024 by Belinda Stevens

All rights reserved. No part of this publication may be reproduced, distributed, or transmitted in any form or by any means, including photocopying, recording, or other electronic or mechanical methods, without the prior written permission of the author, except in the case of brief quotations embodied in critical reviews and certain other noncommercial uses permitted by copyright law.

This is a work of fiction. Names, characters, places and incidents either are products of the author's imagination or are used fictitiously. Any resemblance to actual events or locales or persons, living or dead, is entirely coincidental.

Printed in the United States of America

ISBN 979-8-89114-134-6 (hc)
ISBN 979-8-89114-133-9 (sc)
ISBN 979-8-89114-135-3 (e)

Library of Congress Control Number: 2024921898

2024.11.26

MainSpring Books
5901 W. Century Blvd
Suite 750
Los Angeles, CA, US, 90045

www.mainspringbooks.com

"To: The young lawyer who tried the case, my father who taught me to drive and took me to Christmas parades"

PREFACE

June 22, 1957

Emma Jenkins, the Negro cook, slowly walked up the hill toward the ten-room house. The June heat was unrelenting even at 5:30 in the afternoon. The cook had been working for the Ferriday family for a number of years, long before Michael came to live with his grandmother. Mrs. Ferriday was a sweet lady, and Emma was fond of her employer, but she couldn't say the same thing for her teenaged grandson. He was scary. His frequent tantrums and lack of respect for those who denied him what he wanted angered her. The rage he carried just below the surface made Emma afraid for the boy's grandmother. Michael Ferriday was like a spoiled four-year-old but much larger.

Emma came to the house every afternoon at 5:30 to prepare the evening meal. As she climbed the hill, she considered what she would make for supper, fried chicken, lima beans, and fried okra. Leftover apple pie with

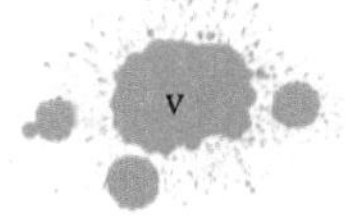

vanilla ice cream would be perfect for dessert. She hoped the grandson wouldn't break any plates.

The uncertainty of his erratic behavior unnerved her. She had raised her own children, and none of them acted like Michael. If they had, she would have taken a belt to them. As she neared the house, she heard shrieking and hammering.

Emma ran up the steps to the front door. What she saw sickened her.

CHAPTER ONE

The sun beat down on Michael's head in waves, causing the sweat to cover his entire head, neck, and upper body. It felt like his brain, along with his body, had melted into the scorching pavement below. The middle of June in the lower Mississippi Delta was like Satan's armpit, at least that is the way the people of the County referred to it.

The smell of hot tar and the sauna-like atmosphere made the seventeen-year-old's stomach lurch. He and his friends had been working for the electric company, repairing power lines, since he graduated from high school. The sticky bun and black coffee he picked up from Newman's store earlier rolled out of his mouth in chewed bits and mushy vomit. He put his head between his legs to stop the spinning while his co-workers chuckled softly and called him not-so-kind names.

The heat and the long hours had taken their toll on Michael, along with the whiskey he had consumed the night before. He knew the liquor was no good for him. But it seemed the only way to survive the hellish

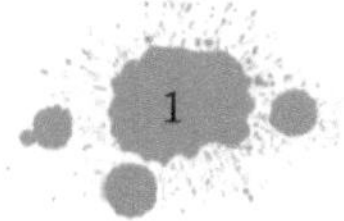

atmosphere that was now part of his existence. So different from the spring of his senior year in high school – that spring had been one of the happiest times of his young life.

He made up his mind that this was the last day he would endure the heat and humiliation. He gave a sullen notice to the foreman, jumped in the front seat of his grandmother's vehicle, and gunned the engine.

As he rounded the curves on Highway 433, he gathered speed to 65 miles an hour and was taking the curves on two wheels. By the time he turned onto Highway 3, Michael realized he was about to have one of his fits. Others called them tantrums, but he couldn't control it, no matter what others called it.

The slamming of the kitchen door made Emma practically jump out of her skin. Michael was shrieking, with a wild look in his eyes. She had seen this behavior before. It was one of Michael's infamous tantrums. Suddenly, he fell to the floor and began to convulse. These spasms went on long enough for Emma to scream for Mrs. Ferriday, who was in the back bedroom of the house.

Some thought his fits were attempts to get his way, while others thought they were evidence of an unbalanced mind.

Michael had lived with his grandmother for twelve months. His mother divorced his father when Michael was nine, then she moved back to town. Michael's relationship with Lisa Ferriday was rocky at best. After years of listening to her son scream, "You don't love me," and enduring his endless fits, Michael's behavior had taken a toll on her mental well-being. Lisa sent Michael to live with her mother. Two years later his paternal grandmother, Lena Ferriday, took over. He spent his senior year in her ten-room house twenty miles outside of the town where he grew up. Both the county and the town bore the same name. It was Indian, and it meant death.

The drive from the town to the house on the hill was not one you would want to brave late at night. The thick foliage came right up to the road with no real easement. There were no lights to guide the way. The land was flat and heavy, like much of the Mississippi Delta. Despite the ominous atmosphere, Michael traveled the road with increased frequency. The reason for his many trips was a girl. She didn't live in the county and wasn't part of his senior class. Even though they had just met, he fell deeply in love. The relationship was a bone of contention between Michael and his grandmother.

Lena Ferriday was a small lady in height and width, a petite woman who wore glasses that were large for her small face. Her eyes denoted a gentleness that the large frames could not hide or change. Her long thin face had a wide mouth that easily broke into a soft smile. Her gray hair was short and neatly styled, framing her face with soft curls.

By the time she entered the kitchen, the tantrum was subsiding. "I quit!" Michael seethed. "You can't make me work. I'm not your trash. I want to go to Marion Institute!" Tears welled up in his eyes and he began sobbing.

Lena's face was transformed into fear and hurt. Those gentle eyes filled with tears. "You're beginning to sound like a broken record," said the grandmother. "I have explained why it's not possible." She begged Michael. "Please, be reasonable."

"NO!," he shouted as he stormed out the kitchen door, slamming it so hard he almost broke it off its hinges. In dismay, the grandmother shook her head, telling Emma she couldn't take much more.

"I'm at my wit's end. Ever since he graduated, he's been uncontrollable. I thought work would calm him down. I was wrong." Emma looked on in sympathy and added, "Yes mam, you need help. That boy's too big to spank."

"I'm going to call his daddy, and see what my son can do," Lena said as she headed toward the hall phone.

Her frustration grew. The line was busy, as usual. "Probably took it off the hook," she thought. Her son, Michael "Mike" Ferriday Sr., was one of three children, yet he acted like an only child. Lena realized she had spoiled her offspring. Her son turned out to be an irresponsible man. He was a mean drunk who left it to others to raise his only child. Her grandson, Michael, was a handsome, yet precocious, teenager who in recent months had become increasingly unbalanced, angry, and unmanageable. So different from the young man who excelled during his last two years of high school.

Michael was never easy. He was a bit of a bully and a total cut-up in class. Early into his junior year, he quit playing football and became serious about his studies. He joined the annual staff, the Rotary Club, was a class officer, and was a straight-A student. He still played baseball – it took less time on the practice field than football. Near the end of his senior year, he was offered a 1958 alternative appointment to West Point. It gave rise to his "delusions of grandeur." He daydreamed of becoming a military leader with untold riches at his disposal.

But no one besides his twelfth-grade English teacher praised him or encouraged him to greatness. A bit of a character, Mrs. Parks alternated between entertaining tales that stretched the truth to making uncompromising demands for excellence from those she taught. Her students loved her and credited her with many of their later successes. An institution who taught generations of young minds, she was vain enough to dye her hair jet black, when it should have been gray. She inspired Michael and won his youthful admiration.

After graduation, Michael missed his teacher, and he missed the companionship of his school friends and the recognition of others. Sometimes he felt special, yet sometimes he felt worthless. The praise he enjoyed in high school evaporated after he graduated. He was left with a grandmother who denied him what he wanted.

The girl was at the heart of the matter. Michael met Betty at the end of his senior year. Over the weeks during May and June, his intense feelings toward her grew. Michael talked of nothing but how much he loved Betty and wanted to marry her. She was beautiful, like Michael's mother, and somewhat sophisticated, which was another reason his grandmother objected to his involvement with the girl. She said he was too young to be so involved with someone. Even the cook advised him to get an education before thinking of marriage. Lena tried to reason with Michael. Finally, she refused him the use of her vehicle and demanded that Michael break it off with Betty.

In the weeks that followed the tension grew between the grandmother and Michael. He began to hear voices, which he says were the almighty talking directly to him. The Lord told Michael he had to do something to be forgiven, to free himself from what he could no longer stand.

Michael grew sullen and unresponsive. Any attempts to talk to him caused hateful glares and stony silence. It was his grandmother's habit to retire early. She always left her car keys on the hall table. Michael stole the keys some nights after she had gone to bed, sneaking out of the house to meet the girl at a designated spot that was secluded and away from prying eyes.

The last time Michael and Betty met, sex was on their minds. They necked to the music of Fats Dominio and Lloyd Price on the car radio. His kisses were fierce, and the girl began to moan when he grabbed her breast. Their clothes were quickly discarded. There was little foreplay. Intercourse was swift and explosive. They rested in each other's arms before starting again.

Betty asked Michael about his grandmother. "Have you talked to her about us?" she asked. "Did you tell her about our plans?"

"I tried to, but she wouldn't listen," he replied. "She insisted we break up, which is something I will never do."

"Baby, what are we going to do?" she asked. "We aren't old enough to get married on our own."

Michael said, "I will ask my daddy. He will help us."

"But your grandmother is your guardian," the girl responded. He quickly interrupted and said, "I don't care! I'll talk to my daddy. He'll help us." His voice softened. "Now kiss me."

He took a swig from a pint of whiskey and then offered it to her.

CHAPTER TWO

The next morning Lena confronted Michael over breakfast. She broke the silence after the eggs and bacon had been consumed. Taking a sip of her orange juice, she informed her grandson that she knew he had taken the car.

"I know you've been stealing my keys and sneaking out to meet up with that girl."

"So, what if I am," he sneered.

"Son, she is nothing but trouble."

Michael interrupted her by yelling, "You can't stop me."

The grandmother responded by saying, "From now on, the keys will be locked up in my bedside table."

"What if I want to see my mother or hang out with my friends?" he asked.

His grandmother thought for a moment and said, "You may use the car between the hours of eight a.m., and seven p.m. No more nightly excursions, no more meeting that girl," she insisted. Suddenly, Michael had a wild look in his eyes. He slammed the table and screamed at his grandmother.

"You bitch!"

She rose from the large dining room table and sighed. With great difficulty, she told her grandson that he must leave her home. "I can't take your tantrums anymore. I'm tired of fighting with you, and I'm tired of the hateful things you say to me. Maybe you should move back in with your mother or with your other grandmother."

"You don't love me," he screamed.

"Yes, I do. But I can't live like this. I'm sixty-seven years old and you're so young and so angry. I need peace. I'm too old to deal with you."

"You don't love me," he repeated, red-faced.

"You're angry," she insisted.

"Nobody loves me," he sobbed. "You want to get rid of me, like everyone else." He then demanded the keys. "I want to be left alone and think."

As he left the house on the hill, he sent gravel flying in all directions. He knew where he could get liquor. The county was dry, but the local bootlegger would sell it to him, even though he was underaged. He wanted to get good and drunk. Knee-walking, grass pulling drunk.

He found a secluded spot on the Vicksburg Road to consume his beers (and a good bit of whiskey). He then called his mother on a pay phone to scream at her.

His hands were shaking as he dialed the number. "You don't love me," he shouted into the phone.

"What?" It took a moment for his mother to realize it was her son on the line.

"I said you don't love me, Mom. Nobody does."

"Son, where are you?"

"I'm not going to tell you," he seethed. "You hate me, just like everyone else."

"You're slurring your words..."

Red-faced, he slammed down the phone. Michael started to leave but went back and dialed again. His mother noticed the second ring. "I'm sick," he said. "I'm seriously ill. I may faint!"

Panicked, Lisa said, "Son, tell me where you are!" But it did no good. Michael hung up again. Five minutes later, he redialed and told his mother he was coming to see her. "I'll be there soon, but I have to make another stop first."

"Where are you going?" Lisa was growing more desperate. "None of your damn business," he yelled.

Michael jumped in the car and headed to the Presbyterian church. He walked up the steps of the red brick building and turned left. He went directly to the minister's study. As he entered, he noticed a wall mirror prominently displayed on the wall. He examined his own image in the mirror, his enlarged pupils and his colorless skin. He couldn't stand to look at himself. In an act of self-hate, he snatched the mirror from the wall and threw it to the ground, smashing the glass into hundreds of shimmering shards.

God had left Michael to suffer unbearable pain. The Lord's voice commanded him to act. He had to escape the darkness, the unrelenting torture. He grabbed a piece of paper and a pencil and began to write a short note to his pastor.

Please ask God to have mercy on my soul. I love God and he knows I love him. I believe in God, but he has punished me more than I can stand. Please pray for me because I want to go to heaven. I know you don't love me, but I love you because you can help me with God. You will never see me again. But please say kind and loving things about me. I will always love my mother and daddy, even though they don't love me. Ask God to have mercy on me, please.

Michael left the note on the pastor's desk and rushed to his vehicle. He raced down the street to his maternal grandmother's residence.

Later, the pastor entered his study to find the shattered mirror and a desperate note on his desk. He called the police, who did a thorough search of the church and the pastor's study. Believing that Michael wanted to kill himself, the pastor attempted to call Lena. He was told by the switchboard operator that the line was busy, that the phone was probably off the hook.

Michael was already driving erratically when he arrived at his grandmother's house in town. Both his mother and maternal grandmother rushed to meet him at the front door. They became even more anxious when they saw the wild look in Michael's eyes. It portrayed a total disconnect from reality. There was nothing normal about his actions or the way he looked.

Sweating and slurring his words, there was a smell of liquor on his breath. But it was more than his intoxicated state that bothered both women. It was his crazy talk that frightened them. Later, his maternal grandmother told others she wished she had called the police.

"I'm pretty sure I've got cancer, my stomach is hurting, and my head feels like someone took an axe to it," he said. Michael's mother took him gently by the shoulders and said, "Come sit down, you look awful."

"I'm going to die, I know it," he said, as he staggered toward the living room sofa. "I've got a tumor in my head. God gave it to me and told me that it would kill me if I didn't change."

"The Lord spoke to you?" asked his grandmother, thinking Michael had taken leave of his senses.

"I can't live there anymore," he screamed, his eyes brimming with tears. His hands began to shake. Jerky movements took over the rest of his body. His grandmother was afraid he would fall on the floor and begin to convulse. "I can't live with that bitch anymore," he wailed.

"Son, what are you talking about?" asked Lisa, who brought him a glass of water and an aspirin. He knocked the glass out of her hand, shattering it to pieces on the floor. Lisa screamed as he pushed her out of the way. He ran to the front door and yelled, "You'll never see me again!" Within an instant, he jumped into the car and took off.

Both women stood speechless, wondering what had just happened. They knew they needed to do something, but they weren't sure just what that was. Michael headed out of town, toward the ten-room house on the hill. As he turned toward Highway 433, he slowed to twenty-five miles an hour. Suddenly, he slammed his foot on the accelerator and went from twenty-five to sixty-five miles an hour within seconds. Others saw the vehicle swaying from side to side as he raced towards the wooden Colonial-style home with blue shutters – a house he wanted to destroy, along with its inhabitants.

He turned off the highway and slowly drove up the hill to his destination. His mind was racing, edging quickly toward insanity. He grabbed two weapons secured from various locations inside the house before heading to the back bedroom where his grandmother lay on her bed, reading the newspaper. He heard a voice telling him what he must do to relieve the pain in his head.

As he entered the bedroom, Lena looked up. Her expression turned from a curious look to one of fear. He screamed, a guttural, animal sound, and raced toward her.

CHAPTER THREE

Lena raised her hands in defense and screamed. "No!"

She tried to reach his right arm, the one he used to hold the revolver. Michael pushed her hands away and struck her in the face with the gun. She fought hard for her life, but he was too strong. He beat her with a pipe, then shot her twice with the revolver. Then he did more damage to her body with a blast of a shotgun.

He wrecked her bedroom, smashing the bed, the bedside table, the lamp, and literally every other object in the room. He dragged her nearly nude and bloodied body into another room. He methodically destroyed each room in the ten-room house. He broke the glass television screen. The refrigerator was overturned. In every room, chairs and tables were smashed against the floors and walls. Every piece of China was shattered into pieces. He hammered every object that made the ten-room house a home. When he was done, he proceeded to inflict further damage to his grandmother's body. Ungodly screeches and howls erupted from deep within him. Sounds that would cause a normal person's blood to run cold.

His last act after slaughtering his grandmother and destroying her home was to take her diamond ring, as well as what money she had. Michael had consumed five beers and a half-pint of whiskey. Naked and in a drunken state, he passed out in the only bedroom he didn't destroy.

As Emma climbed the steps to the house, she heard Michael's screams and hammering. She rushed to the door and saw the mutilated body of the grandmother lying in the hallway. Horrified, she ran down the hill and across the highway to a local store. Weeping, she was barely able to get the words out. She told the owner what she had seen.

"Oh Lord," Emma gasped between sobs. "That sweet lady! I worked for that family for years. She certainly didn't deserve what he did to her. Oh, her body."

The store's owner got a glass of water and offered it to the hysterical cook. "You're going to have to calm down," he said. "You have to tell the Sheriff all you have seen and heard. I've called him, and he is on his way."

"Okay," she mumbled. "You know she volunteered at the hospital," she added.

The store owner agreed the grandmother was, indeed, a nice lady, beloved throughout the community. He shuddered when he thought about what that boy had done to her.

Twenty miles away, a wedding was about to take place. The groom and best man were in the pastor's study when he received the call telling him about the murder. The church was filled with family members and friends of Lena Ferriday's.

The groom and his best man made the decision not to tell the bride about the murder so it wouldn't ruin her day. Yet before the day was over, everyone in the community was buzzing with the news. One of Michael's cousins later said the wedding of her close friend and the murder of Lena Ferriday would always be tied together in her mind.

The first to arrive at the house on the hill was a neighbor and the local funeral director, arriving before the Sheriff. Neither entered the wrecked home until the Sheriff arrived around six p.m. The Sheriff and his two deputies entered the house, followed by the funeral director. First, they viewed the mutilated body of the grandmother. Next, they went from room to room, taking in the horrific damage done to the home. Photographs were taken of the grisly crime scene. Both deputies almost threw up upon seeing the carnage. When they entered the kitchen, one of the deputies called out to the Sheriff.

"Boss, look what he did to the refrigerator. How in the hell did he have the strength to push it over?" The deputy shook his head in disbelief. The Sheriff surveyed the damage and also shook his head. The Sheriff found the shotgun, revolver, and a blood-stained pipe. Later he told others what he saw in that house shook him to his very core. "Never, in all my years, have I witnessed anything so horrible. That boy is a monster!"

When they moved to the front bedroom, the men found the naked body of the seventeen-year-old boy lying face-down on the bed. He had not moved since he passed out drunk. The Sheriff shook him hard to try to rouse him. If Michael had offered any resistance, the older man probably would have beaten him to death. The Sheriff found the grandmother's diamond ring and some cash in his bloody clothes. It was obvious he planned to escape but passed out instead. The Sheriff shouted, "Why did you do this?" Groggy, Michael looked up and mumbled, "Wah?"

"Why in the name of God did you do this to your grandmother?" the Sheriff demanded. Michael began to quietly weep.

"She wouldn't let me go to Marion Institute. She tried to make me break up with the girl I love. I couldn't allow that."

"So, you slaughtered her and wrecked her house?"

"I don't remember," Michael cried, wiping his eyes. "I want to die. I'm ready to die."

"Boy, I'll do my best to see that you do." With that, both deputies jerked Michael to his feet. They threw a blanket over him and dragged him to the backseat of the Sheriff's cruiser. On the way, they made Michael take another look at his dead and broken grandmother. He let out a howl and screamed," I want to die! God, have mercy on me!"

The funeral director arranged to have the body transported to the local hospital for examination. The doctor who performed the examination received his training in a MASH unit during the Korean War.

It didn't take long for the entire community to feel either fear or hatred toward Michael. The rage the people felt never really lessened, even years later. They remembered him as a mean bully, a deranged demon.

As the Sheriff's cruiser pulled away from the house on the hill, Michael looked back and realized it was the last time he would see the house that he destroyed. He began to sober up and realized the terrible thing he had done. Later, he told his lawyer that his grandmother was the only person he really loved.

He was taken to the Sheriff's office for further questioning where Michael once again admitted to killing his grandmother and his reasons for doing so. The Sheriff asked Michael if he'd put his statement in writing. "No!" Michael said emphatically.

"Son, you have already admitted to what you have done. Why not put your confession on paper?" Again, Michael shouted, "No! I want a lawyer. Let me talk to my daddy!"

"Your father is out of town, and we haven't been able to reach him," said the Sheriff. "Your cousin and your mother are here. Do you want to talk with them?"

"No! Tell them to get me a lawyer!" As Michael was processed and fingerprinted, the Sheriff met with Lisa. He invited her into the privacy of the deputy's office.

"I'm so sorry. I wish we were meeting under different circumstances. Your son has given a statement saying that he killed his grandmother. After he's been processed, a doctor will examine him." Lisa, on the verge of hysteria, interrupted the Sheriff and demanded to see her son. "He doesn't want to see you," the Sheriff said. "He only asked for his daddy. He said to tell you to hire a lawyer for him."

Three hours later, Michael was examined by the same doctor who examined the body of his dead grandmother. No one dared to question his findings. Michael was sent to a community hospital, the same hospital where his grandmother Lena had served as a volunteer.

CHAPTER FOUR

The moment the doctor entered the examination room, he could smell the overpowering odor of alcohol. He asked Michael if he had anything in his system.

"Yes," Michael admitted. "I have four beers and half a pint of whiskey."

"What about drugs," questioned the doctor. "Do you have drugs in your system?"

Michael answered quietly, "No, I don't use drugs."

The doctor explained to Michael that a tech would come in to draw blood after the examination, Michael began to shake and sweat profusely, and screamed, "No! No one can touch me. No one but you!" While his pulse and heart rate were checked, Michael told his childhood physician he wanted to die. He cried out, "I'm not afraid, so go ahead and kill me. I did wrong, and I'm ready to be punished."

As the doctor was taking blood from Michael's left arm, he noticed scratches on both arms. The red marks traveled from his wrists all the way up to his shoulders. Suddenly, the doctor realized his grandmother had fought hard for her life. As Michael observed the look in the doctor's eyes, he screamed, "I want to die!" When the doctor asked why he felt that way, he said, "I killed someone." The doctor took his time, asking Michael, "Who did you kill?" Michael sobbed uncontrollably as he answered the doctor. "My grandmother."

After the doctor drew Michael's blood, he gave him a shot to tranquilize him.

"Tell me what happened," the doctor said calmly. "And tell me how you got those bloody marks on your arms."

"I don't remember. I was drunk."

"You mean you blacked out?"

"Yes."

"Tell me what you remember."

"Only entering my grandmother's bedroom. I was angry. I was covered by a red mist. That's all I remember."

"Nothing else?" The doctor tried to get Michael to open up but had no success. When the exam was over, Michael was transferred to the county jail. The jailor brought him something to eat, and Michael sniffed at the food and took a bite. Suddenly, he threw the tin plate across the room.

"Are you trying to poison me? You son-of-a-bitch!" Michael shouted as the jailer backed out of the cell and left the contents of Michael's supper on the floor. When visitors arrived, the jailor warned them to be careful. "That boy is as mean as a rattlesnake."

At ten o'clock that night, the authorities were finally able to locate Michael's father, Michael Ferriday Sr., who goes by Mike. He had just arrived home from Vicksburg when his phone rang. The Sheriff asked him to come to the Courthouse. When Mike arrived, the solemn-faced Sheriff ushered him into his office.

"What's this all about, Sheriff?"

"At five-thirty this afternoon, your son murdered your mother."

Mike let out a huge breath, then shouted, 'What?"

"That's right. Your son murdered your mother this afternoon, and he destroyed her home."

"Wait a minute," Mike said. "What the hell are you saying, Sheriff? That can't be right."

Suddenly Mike, ashen faced, went into shock, hyperventilating and crying at the same time. After receiving medical attention, the Sheriff called in the local doctor who gave him a shot for his extreme anxiety. The Sheriff went on to tell Mike about the state of his mother's body and about the shattered contents of the home, and how he found Michael passed out in the front bedroom.

"Are you sure my son was responsible?"

The Sheriff explained that besides the physical evidence, they had the cook's statement. "There's also Michael's admission."

"Did he provide a written statement?"

"No," the Sheriff said. "He refused to sign anything and wants you to hire an attorney for him."

"Sheriff, may I see my son now?"

Michael was sitting in the corner with a copy of the New Testament in his hands when Mike entered the cell. Michael put the Bible down and raced into his father's arms. Both began sobbing. After the brief visit, Mike agreed to hire an attorney for Michael.

He actually hired two attorneys, both of whom had stellar reputations for winning cases. The townsfolk called them "The Gold Dust Twins" due to their ability to win the most difficult of cases. The head counsel, John Mason, was the son of a federal judge. He made his money through personal injury and his reputation for defending murder cases. A fairly young man of forty, he was the father of two boys and two girls. Little did he know a fifth child was on its way.

John Mason was a shy man with a dry sense of humor, although he was not shy in the Courtroom, where he dazzled people with his eloquence. He often said the practice of law was a privilege, not a right. He told his daughter to always return phone calls, be honest, and work hard at whatever she did. She later said her father reminded her of Atticus Finch from *To Kill a Mockingbird*. Like Finch, he cared deeply for his clients. Emotionally and physically, his murder cases took years off his life.

When Michael's father contacted him, he wasn't sure he wanted to handle the case - not only because of its brutality but Michael himself added to the attorney's reluctance. The seventeen-year-old was the same age as the attorney's oldest child. Michael played football with his son. It was just too close to home. He felt pity for Michael. He wasn't sure he could keep his emotions at bay and do a good job. John was glad he had a second chair. Co-counsel for the case was Jeffrey Bennett, who was not without his own talents. Jeffrey was someone who could easily handle any challenge that might arise. The attorney knew he had his work cut out for him. His first act was to meet with his new client.

Before entering the cell, the jailor warned the attorney about his temperamental client. Michael was anything but confrontational. He sat in the corner, his eyes downcast, his hands holding a copy of the New Testament. Michael rose when he saw John Mason and held out his hand for a handshake. Michael thanked his lawyer for taking on his case. They talked briefly of possible witnesses for and against the defense and what little facts Michael could share. After a thirty-minute interview, John left to meet with Jeffrey.

Later, there were more visitors to the jail. A handful of friends and Michael's maternal grandmother, Carol Spruill, came to see Michael. He told his grandmother that God had spoken to him numerous times, even in his jail cell. Michael's auditory hallucinations and bizarre dreams caused serious concern for Carol. She contacted John Mason about Michael's mental state.

Things got worse. Michael's strange behavior and grim references to death caused the Sheriff to search the jail cell. What he found raised alarm with the attorney, as well as with Michael's family. A razor blade was discovered in the middle of the New Testament. Upon making that discovery, the Sheriff instituted strict security measures pertaining to Michael's person and his immediate surroundings.

Michael's erratic behavior did not end with the razor. He attempted to contact his former English teacher, Mrs. Parks, asking for her help. Her response wasn't encouraging. She sent him a note:

I'm sorry. There is nothing I can do. I will pray for you.

Not to be discouraged, he wrote a very strange letter to his beloved teacher:

> *I received your note, and I certainly appreciate it. You said there was nothing you could do, physically, but there is. You probably understood me and know my weaknesses mentally more than anyone. I know God gave me a very dull, ignorant, and normal mind. But I feel that as long as I am living I must cultivate and improve this mind to the very limit of its dull power. I pray for death for myself but as long as I am living my only chance will be to sharpen my mind until it is as sharp as it can possibly be.*
>
> *I had a wonderful dream and in this dream, God said I was doomed for either fabulous wealth or success or death. I pray for death, for I know it is not humanly possible for me to live a happy, satisfied, and contended life unless this fabulous dream was to come true. I either want the life I dream of or death. <u>I want no normal life</u>.*
>
> *I would greatly appreciate any advice you could give me to help sharpen my mind while I'm living under these circumstances. Maybe you could send me a list of the <u>very top books for my mind</u>. I would appreciate it.*
>
> *I feel as though it is my duty to God as long as I am living, since he <u>gave me no talent</u>, to take this weak mind and build it until it has reached its sharpest and top point.*
>
> *I write this letter to you because I think you are the wisest person in the world as far as knowing my strong points and weaknesses. I beg you to help me mentally. I love you and please pray for my death.*
>
> *P.S. Please help me mentally. I must be smart as it is my only chance. Please answer my letter and help me mentally to be razor-sharp.*
>
> *God bless you.*

The letter was dated July 6, 1957. It was two weeks after the murder. Mrs. Parks forwarded the letter to his attorney. She, like so many others, was worried about Michael's mental state. Later, Michael's communication with his teacher would be made public.

CHAPTER FIVE

After the discovery of the razor in Michael's Bible, security at the jail was increased. Two deputies watched Michael like a hawk. The jailor's dislike of Michael increased, along with his fear of him. He refused to have any contact with Michael without others present, preferably one of the two deputies.

Lead counsel John Mason requested the teenager be examined by the chief psychiatrist at the State Mental Hospital. The seventeen-year-old was examined several times, during two-hour intervals. The prognosis of Michael's disease was not good. He was diagnosed as paranoid schizophrenic with little or no hope of recovery. His attorneys were not satisfied with what they were told. John sought a second opinion. He was given the name of a doctor who was renowned in forensic medicine. With numerous medical degrees and studies under his belt, the psychiatrist was respected throughout the county for his treatment of the criminally insane. He taught at Tulane University in New Orleans, which provided easy access to Michael.

Meanwhile, Carol and Lisa became increasingly worried about Michael. Carol asked for a special meeting with John Mason. She wanted to speak to the young attorney representing her grandson. In the John's dusty law office, Carol expressed her concerns. The law office had not been updated since the 1930s. The lighting consisted of shaded lamps scattered throughout the office. The blinds covering the windows were yellowed with age. The antique desk and leather chairs offered some attempt at decoration, along with pictures of the lawyer's grandfather, a United States senator, and his father, an acting Federal judge. Carol lowered her head and began to cry.

"My grandson is getting worse. My visits with him have become increasingly stressful. Half the time, he stares off into the distance. He rocks back and forth, moaning, sometimes howling out loud. Other times he tells me about his conversations with God, who he says tells him about either a fabulous future or certain death. He tells me he doesn't know what will happen. But he says God told him to prepare for a fabulous future by changing himself mentally. Michael gave me a list of books he wanted me to get for him. He says he must educate himself by reading as much as possible."

John reached out and patted the woman's hands in an attempt to comfort her. He advised her to keep her communication with Michael even. "Get these books for him. Ask your grandson why he wants to read these books. Ask him about his conversations with God. There is a lot we can learn from what he says. It will help him in the long run."

"Okay," said Carol. "I'll do my best."

"Don't worry. I'll do everything I can to help your grandson. And a few prayers won't hurt."

Carol lifted her head and said, "Yes sir, thank you." She left, head down and tears still in her eyes.

John met with Michael's mother, Lisa, numerous times. He learned in excruciating detail the abuse she suffered from her ex-husband. She told the lawyer what her son saw during those days which she described as a living hell.

"My son saw his father kick me in the stomach and bloody my nose. He saw numerous acts of abuse by his father when my husband was drunk.

The rage he showed when he was drunk was so frightening. I divorced Mike to save my life. I knew he would kill me if I remained married to him."

John talked to other members of the family, including Michael's aunts, father, and first cousin. He received various contradictory remarks concerning the sanity of the seventeen-year-old. His aunts and first cousins declared that he acted sane. They said he was a typical teenager who played sports and liked girls. Neither his aunts nor his first cousin, who saw him every day after school, reported expressions of rage. None saw his anger or desperation. According to them, he was just a youngster looking forward to graduation and an unlimited future which included West Point.

The lawyer's interviews with Michael's teachers, his principal, and the superintendent of education offered little other than basic observations that Jeffrey had already known or guessed.

The young attorney viewed the wreckage of the ten-room house that Michael destroyed on the day he allegedly murdered his grandmother. The Ferriday family had already started proceedings to sell the house and the land surrounding it. As John viewed the shattered wood and broken glass, as well as blood stains everywhere, he realized no one would ever live in that house again. Later, rumors would spread that the spirit of the murdered woman roamed from room to room, gazing at the destruction her grandson had created. Next, John spoke with the Sheriff and his deputies who relayed the grisly sight they saw when they reached the crime scene. They told the young attorney how they felt -- the anger they had after viewing the victim's nude and battered body. John then spoke with the funeral director who told him the family couldn't have an open casket at the service. He told John how Michael literally destroyed the face of his paternal grandmother.

Lastly, John interviewed the doctor who examined the corpse shortly after the murder. He showed the young lawyer photographs of the mutilated body, including the unrecognizable lower parts of the elderly woman. For the first time in his legal career, the husband and father of four felt deep sorrow for everyone concerned. He also felt sick to his stomach.

Back in the confines of his office, John put his head in his hands and winched at the pain he suddenly felt for Michael and for the elderly woman who was murdered. Later he met with co-counsel to plan their defense.

CHAPTER SIX

After meeting with his co-counsel, John Mason contacted a New Orleans psychiatrist and asked for recent studies on paranoid schizophrenia. He spent hours that ran into days, then weeks, of research. He learned that the condition Michael suffered from started in childhood; probably brought on by his father's alcoholic behavior. John discovered the disorder usually manifests itself in the late teens or early twenties.

John contacted some of Michael's peers who were willing to talk to him. He had no intention of putting the young men on the stand. He only wanted to understand Michael better. He wanted to see if there were symptoms of schizophrenia early on. What he discovered astounded him. The fits and delusions of grandeur Michael had in his late teens occurred long before his grandmother's murder. As one teen explained: "He thought more of himself than others did."

"What do you mean," asked the John.

"He thought he was better than everyone else. Superior."

"What else did you observe?"

"He had no control. He played baseball with me. If he made an error, he would throw a fit."

"Not very sportsmanlike was it," John remarked.

"No sir. It went against what our coaches tried to instill in us."

Another young friend told the attorney about Michael's bullying ways that went back to elementary school.

"He would pick on boys smaller than him. I didn't like it when he did that. It was like he was two different people."

"Anything else?" John asked.

"Yes. He would expose himself to little girls. It was upsetting to see," explained Michael's friend.

John believed that much of this abnormal behavior was directly related to his father, and that Michael thought it was normal and right. To become enraged was okay. To bully and mistreat others who were weaker than you was fine. It was what Michael observed when his father brutalized his mother.

The youth of the town were shocked, even horrified, by what they had learned. Most had grown up naïve and innocent to the realities of the dark side of the 1950s. Most came from middle-class neighborhoods where no one locked their doors at night. Girls went to college to get an "MRS" degree. If a girl did seek a career after college, it was as a nurse or a teacher. Most hoped to receive an engagement ring during their senior year and follow in the footsteps of their mothers and grandmothers. Sex before marriage was frowned upon. And drugs were nonexistent among the youth of the fifties. It was in this atmosphere that the grisly murder of a grandmother exploded onto the scene.

News of the horrific crime spread beyond the confines of the town. It expanded from one end of the state to the other. It was in every newspaper from *The Commercial Appeal* in Memphis to *The Times Picayune* in New Orleans. Television broadcasters as well as newspaper reporters attempted to interview the seventeen-year-old in his jail cell. Mike, who seemed to thrive on the publicity, encouraged Michael's public exposure while the lead counsel did his best to prevent access to his client.

As time marched toward a very public trial, the attorney grew disgusted with the sensational press, as well as with Michael's father. When the gory aspects of Lena Ferriday's murder came to light, John became anxious about the reaction of the public. It became more difficult to find unbiased jurors who didn't feel Michael should get the gas chamber.

The youth of the town were the most traumatized by the murder. Most knew Michael and found it hard to believe that he would do such a thing. There were others, however, who were not at all surprised. Some felt guilty over not expressing concern about his previous behavior. And there were those who wanted him to kill himself and release the town from the horror he had created. Some feared him, others hated him. It was in this atmosphere that John Mason would try his case, to attempt to save his client from a death sentence. Long before the first day of trial, he realized that the best defense for Michael was insanity.

The lawyer had to convince the jury, and the town itself, that Michael did not know what he was doing. That he didn't understand the concepts of right and wrong at the time of the murder. During his arraignment, Michael waived the reading of the indictment and said, "Not guilty." Counsels for the defense asked for, and received a continuance, so their star witness could be in Court to testify. The Judge set the trial for the second week of November, shortly before the Thanksgiving holidays.

In the meantime, John Mason and Jeffrey Bennett, as counsels for the defense, went over their research with the chief psychiatrist at State Hospital and the forensic expert from New Orleans. Despite numerous sessions with both, there were still unanswered questions. Since Michael's memory was impaired, he could not recall what exactly happened. Michael was not able to explain what set him off nor could he tell anything about the actual killing. What was it in his psyche that created such rage within him? Was it just below the surface all along, waiting for the right moment to appear? What caused so much hate, so much brutality in one so young? There was no treatment, no medicine, to cure so much anguish. The only solution was to lock him up, perhaps forever. It saddened John to realize the awful waste.

In his jail cell, Michael alternated between streams of a bright future promised by God to the depths of despair. To live, or to kill himself. Those were his choices. His fate was no longer in his hands; however, his continued existence might depend on the State, who wanted him dead.

CHAPTER SEVEN

During the long months between the end of June and early November, Michael's mental state continued to deteriorate as his maternal grandmother became increasingly anxious. Talks with his pastor only increased his belief that God promised Michael untold riches. When he talked with the head counsel, Michael stated he wanted to die, convinced the State was plotting his demise. Talking to a psychiatrist brought out his guilt and memories of the violent atmosphere of his childhood. Nothing and no one could bring him closer to sanity. He alternated from joyful fantasy to deep sadness. Sometimes he would read his Bible, rocking back and forth and sobbing loudly.

His visits with others were scaled down. The only family members he met with were Carol Spruill, his maternal grandmother, and the occasional visit from his father. Friends were no longer allowed, due to the agitation it provoked. He couldn't bear to think about his recent past, his school days, and the present, locked inside a jail cell.

During his brief appearance in Court for his arraignment, Michael sat motionless, his head down, refusing to look at anyone. Sometimes he glanced out the window, but never at the people in the Courtroom. His demeanor was unresponsive and listless. It appeared he had given up on Court proceedings. He felt it was hopeless to believe in a favorable outcome. This made the defense counsel's job twice as difficult.

Their client's refusal to assist in his trial made things harder to deal with. As time passed, the frustration and fear grew on all sides. John Mason tried to reach Michael. He tried to assure him everything was being done for his benefit. He wanted to convince the teenager that he wouldn't die, that he wouldn't spend his young life in prison. Yet his attorney couldn't promise something he wasn't sure of himself. Death penalty cases were hell to try, but this case was the worst. The Sheriff made it clear that Michael must remain isolated from the rest of the prison population. This isolation increased Michael's anguish, along with his insanity -- something John tried to tell the Sheriff.

"No sir. I don't care. I won't endanger the lives of my other prisoners for the sake of your client," the Sheriff stated.

"Sheriff, I can assure you my client will not harm anyone. What he did was an aberration, not to be repeated."

"Tell that to my jailer. He's absolutely terrified of him. I need to put him somewhere else and appoint someone new to guard your oh-so-innocent client."

"This isolation is causing more damage. His mental state is fractured at best."

"And you want me to release a crazy man among other prisoners? No! He's just mean, counselor. Mean as a junkyard dog!"

"Sheriff, my client has more to fear from others than any harm he might inflict on fellow prisoners. Just let him out into the yard for exercise. No socializing."

The Sheriff stood up and slammed his hand down on the metal desk of his examination room. "I said no! Get a Court order if that's what you want."

The young lawyer stood up and extended his hand. The Sheriff shook it, but as he left the room he said,

"I'm sorry you feel that way, Sheriff."

"I'm sorry, too. This case has caused a lot of stress. I didn't mean to take it out on you."

John decided to request a continued suicide watch for his client. He spent more time visiting Michael before the November trial. When the young lawyer visited his client, Michael was usually listless, exhibiting no interest in anything that was said to him. Reaching for straws, the attorney asked, "Tell me about your high school days. I know you played football. I heard you were a good running back." At that point, Michael's face lit up.

"Yes sir," he said. "I was."

The more time they spent together, the closer they became. Michael's respect and admiration for his attorney increased, and John grew in sympathy for the lost boy.

"What if I brought you some books to read," John asked. "Some of my favorites. The Sheriff gave his permission."

At that point, Michael's face lit up. "Yes sir. I would love that."

The notoriety of the pending trial affected not only the attorneys but their families as well. This was especially true of John's teenage son, who played football with Michael. He was a sensitive soul who hid the horror of what he really felt about the crime with bravado and tasteless jokes. His younger sister could see right through his guise. She knew if she broached the subject her brother would deny what he felt. She also knew he was close to his own grandmother and couldn't understand such blatant violence to anyone, much less an elderly woman. He had read the papers and listened to the news. He was haunted by the description of the body and the wrecked house. It was the stuff of nightmares. But he didn't want his father to know. That wouldn't be cool.

John's wife, Kay, realized her children were affected by the case. She did her best to keep the facts from them, especially from the younger children. One evening she asked her older son to meet her in the den adjacent to the master bedroom.

The den was small but cozy. Tall windows lined the walls, covered by gold-colored drapery. Two blue and green oversized armchairs flanked a handsome plaid sofa. A glass-topped coffee table was placed in front of the sofa. An ornately carved wooden desk anchored one side of the room. Kay sat down, patting the sofa cushion next to her.

"Come sit down, son, and tell me what's wrong. I know something's bothering you."

"No Mama, I'm fine."

"I heard you yell out in your sleep last night."

He laughed and said, "From now on, I'll remember to close my bedroom door at night."

"It's that case, isn't it? Please, son, don't lie. It's got everyone unnerved, even your father."

The teenager shook his head, his eyes cast towards the floor. The mother reached out and placed her hand on his hands, folded in his lap.

"Remember the afternoon I had friends over, the guys I played football with?"

"Yes," she laughed. "I don't know how you crammed all those boys in your small bedroom."

"He was one of them. Gives me chills thinking about it. Sis was sitting in the hallway, just a few feet away from my bedroom."

"What happened with his grandmother was an aberration. A once-in-a-lifetime tragedy. It will not happen again," Kay emphasized.

"You can't know that Mama."

"It's not likely son."

The teenager, along with most of the youth of the small town, didn't forget. Decades later they remembered with clarity the murder and that Michael committed it. When the John's son was in his forties, he read Truman Capote's *In Cold Blood* and compared it to the seemingly cold-blooded murder of a grandmother.

CHAPTER EIGHT

While preparing for trial, John Mason depended heavily on his wife. Many considered Kay to be a beautiful woman, comparing her coloring to Snow White's. People didn't realize there was an analytical mind behind those large brown eyes. Kay, like her young daughter, was a keen observer of human nature. Her input was matchless as to the opening statements and closing arguments. She was a great help in drafting questions for various witnesses, including those for and against the defense. As his number one cheerleader, John especially needed Kay during the three months prior to the trial.

Neither Kay nor John wore their feelings on their sleeves, but that didn't mean they didn't feel deeply. Besides the worry the young lawyer felt over the case, he felt other things as well. It unnerved him that Michael was the same age as his oldest son. And like his son, Michael was involved in the same sports and school activities. The two boys had mutual friends, some very close. The similarity between the two caused fear, even sorrow for his client. There was no empathy because it was hard to understand the Michael or identify with him. His own son would follow in John's footsteps and join the Marines. Later he would receive a college degree in business administration. What would happen to Michael if a jury found him "not guilty?" Life in an asylum awaited him where he would be subjected to shock treatment and God knows what else.

The one thing that sustained the attorney was his belief in the rule of law. He considered the United States Constitution a sacred document. He taught his children that it was the basis for America's judicial system and should be honored as such. His classroom was the dinner table, where lively debate and strong opinions were served nightly. John took pleasure in his children's verbal battles. He loved anything that stimulated the mind. Kay, however, didn't appreciate the chaotic clashes among her children. She didn't feel it was good for the nerves or digestion. But the dinner table continued to be the lawyer's most effective learning tool. Even his grandchildren eventually witness to it. The one thing that was not discussed at suppertime was Michael's murder case.

The weeks leading up to the trial consisted of late-night preparation. Weekend golf and tennis games were canceled. The only recreation he allowed himself was dining out with his family on Sundays. His favorite haunt was a local restaurant specializing in fried shrimp and lemon icebox pie. He often joked that his youngest daughter always ate more when they dined out. "She's not a cheap date," he laughed. "The more money spent, the more she eats."

The family pets also brought a sense of normalcy. He walked the family dog, a golden lab, and made a warm bed for the cat on cold nights. The lab was a gift for John's younger child but ended up becoming his pet. John often joked that the dog gave him more respect than the rest of the family. His furry companion lived to be seventeen, and his loyalty to his master paid off. John had an air-conditioning unit installed in the rather large doghouse to ensure the dog's comfort.

The family was everything to John. Without his children, wife, and pets, it is doubtful he would have been as successful. Much like Kay, John was not a social animal. All entertainment, vacation time, and religious worship centered around the family.

Weeks prior to trial, the defense attorneys began their in-depth process of talking with and preparing their witnesses. The first on the list was Emma, the cook who discovered the body. The middle-aged colored woman was terrified by the prospect of testifying in front of twelve white men. She had been trained not to look white people in the face, to respond with fear and deference. The memories of what she had seen still troubled her. At night, she screamed and cried in her sleep. Emma had worked for the grandmother and her husband for years. Her elderly employer had been kind to her, helping her out when it was needed. She was wary of Michael, not knowing what he might do next. What he did was something she never would have imagined until confronted with its gory results. For the rest of her life, Emma would periodically visualize the broken body of Lois Ferriday, the smell of her blood, and the wreckage in the house.

John knew he had to tread carefully while preparing Emma for her testimony in the Courtroom.

"I know this is difficult, but we need to go over your testimony again."

Emma pulled a tissue from her purse. "I don't think I can. Please sir, not again! I've already told the Sheriff everything I know."

"You understand, the State will call you to the stand if I don't. Both sides want to know what you saw. I want to know about Michael's behavior and his relationship with his grandmother," he emphasized.

"I can't live through that again," she wailed.

The young attorney smiled and said softly, "I know this is difficult, but I need, we need, you to go through this again, for the sake of Michael and his grandmother."

"No, please. No," she moaned.

He reached out and patted her shaking hands and assured her. "I'll be right there with you. We'll go over the process until you're comfortable with it. I won't let anyone badger or upset you while you're on the stand." He looked directly into her eyes and said, "Do you believe me?"

"Yes sir."

Several hours later, they were finished. As Emma was getting ready to leave, he told her to simply tell the truth. "And remember, if anyone asks you something you don't understand, ask them to repeat it and to explain the question, okay?"

"Yes sir, I'll remember," Emma said as she headed out the door.

The next two witnesses were equally daunting. Michael's mother, Lisa, and her mother, Carol Spruill, were extremely emotional when it came to Michael. They had a range of feelings from guilt to extreme fear. The two women blamed themselves for not recognizing how sick Michael was and for not getting him the help he needed. They feared that their only son and grandson would die, murdered by the State. John dreaded their pain, as well as the difficult, unanswerable questions they would ask them during the sessions.

CHAPTER NINE

Michael's mother, Lisa Ferriday, would be one of the most heart-wrenching witnesses for the defense. The beautiful, relatively young woman had endured a violent and life-threatening marriage. Now she was facing the possible death of her only son.

Lisa worked for a local car dealership ever since her divorce from Mike Ferriday. When she entered the dusty office of John Mason, she had the look of one who had lost all hope. Her beauty was marred by swollen eyes and a red nose caused by the shedding of many tears. There were looks of sympathy on the faces of the attorney and his secretary as she was ushered into the inner office and told to take a seat in a red leather chair.

John looked at Lisa with kindness. "I know this is difficult, but it's necessary to prepare for your testimony."

"I understand," she said. "It's just so hard to go through all of it, over and over again." Before they could get started, the telephone rang. It was the Emma, hysterical because the District Attorney's office had subpoenaed her. The attorney told her it was okay. Again, he calmed her with his reassurance. As he hung up the telephone, he said, "That was Emma, the cook. The State has subpoenaed her." The color drained from the mother's face as she exclaimed, "Oh no, that's not good. She'll describe what the body looked like."

"It doesn't really hurt us," the attorney explained. "Our defense is insanity. So there's nothing she can say that will prove your son wasn't insane at the time of his grandmother's death."

"If you say so," the mother responded, not completely convinced.

"As a matter of fact, I was thinking of calling her myself," he interjected.

Getting to the reason for the meeting, John asked Lisa to describe how she became involved with Michael's father. The defense counsel wanted details about their marriage and what Michael observed in the home. Just as Lisa began to describe the severe beatings she suffered, Jeffrey Bennett, fresh from a hearing, walked in. After greeting Lisa, he sat down and began to take notes of the young woman's statement. It was hard for both attorneys not to wince as the woman detailed what she endured. They were both experienced trial lawyers and had been subjected to some awful things, but Lisa's description of what she suffered at the hands of her husband was hard to absorb, no matter how many times she repeated it.

As the defense attorneys continued their research, they realized they needed a more recent treatise on mental illnesses. They were missing the latest book published on the subject, a copy of *Clinical Psychology*, which didn't reach them until shortly before the trial. That didn't stop the District Attorney from accusing them of sharing their research material with Michael.

The closer the trial came, the harder the defense counsel worked. Kay worried about her husband's health. John was a heavy smoker and consistently worked long hours, many times late into the night. Kay reminded him of what happened during the first case he ever tried.

"Remember how you fainted in the middle of the trial?"

"I hadn't eaten anything that day," John explained. "It was hunger."

"I'm just saying that you need to take care of yourself. Get enough rest," Kay emphasized as she pointed to the clock on the playroom wall. It was two o'clock in the morning.

As October changed into November, the cold of pre-winter set in. Leaves fell off the trees and Christmas shopping began in earnest. John and Jeffrey started working on questions for a special voir dire, the process where each juror could be questioned individually by both sides. Jurors' backgrounds and possible biases were to be examined. The Circuit Clerk was contacted for background questionnaires for at least one hundred and fifty individuals from the jury pool.

In addition to voir dire questions, there were outlines for opening statements to prepare. There were also pre-trial motions to consider. The anticipation of everyone concerned grew considerably. From the talk around town, several people planned on being in the Courtroom on the morning of November 13, 1957. The judge planned on excluding juveniles from attending the trial. He felt the evidence presented would be too gruesome for the town's young people to hear. Never mind that the gory details of the murder had already appeared in the local newspaper.

Michael sat in his small cell thinking of past Novembers. He could hear the roar of the crowds as the cheerleaders led the football team onto the field. He remembered the pep rallies and the dances after the games. Homecoming had passed, and the town's Thanksgiving parade was happening soon, both without his presence. Some afternoons he could hear the high school band rehearsing *Winter Wonderland* from his jail cell window.

He wondered about his future, and if he would be alive next November. Michael wondered if they would bury him beside his grandparents. He hoped so. He remembered telling his attorney his grandmother was the only person he really loved. The sad thing was he meant it.

His nightly Bible reading helped. But nothing seemed to help the night before his trial. He couldn't get the image of his grandmother out of his mind. The vision of her broken body would stay with him, searing into his brain. He wished the Sheriff's deputies had not forced him to look at her before they dragged him to the cruiser. One minute he wanted to die, the next he wanted to live.

As Michael dressed in a white wool sweater and black slacks the following morning, he felt his stomach flip. The nausea he experienced wouldn't go away. He couldn't eat anything. All he wanted was a Coke to settle his stomach. As he walked into the Courtroom, he looked away from the crowd that had gathered, lowering his head as he walked toward the wooden chair that was to be his seat for the next three days.

CHAPTER TEN

The first day of Court was a dismal disappointment for many curious onlookers who crammed within the overcrowded Courtroom. The early proceedings consisted of a prolonged selection of the jury. It began with the judge educating those who might be selected on what their duties on the jury would be. It was also the judge's responsibility to eliminate those who were too old and infirmed to serve from the jury pool. Certain exclusions included single business owners and caregivers. The judge considered those suffering from chronic conditions that prevented individuals from sitting through many days of trial. Jury selection normally took two to three hours, sometimes longer. It was called "qualifying the jury," and it did not require the attorneys to be present, giving them extra time to look over trial documents. It was also a chance to speak to witnesses before trial – a necessary time for attorneys to calm any nervousness and answer any last-minute questions.

The process continued in earnest after lunch with the voir dire of what was left of the jury pool. The judge explained the process and its necessity. He then introduced the attorneys for the defense and the attorneys from the District Attorney's office. He asked if anyone in the jury pool knew or had dealings with any of the attorneys, including prior clients, family, friends, and those who had official dealings with the District Attorney's office. Then the judge asked if anyone was kin to the young man, friends with him, or just knew him through the community. Numerous hands went up. This slowed down the process since each person was individually questioned for possible bias. Certain people who said they couldn't serve because of preconceived opinions were excused.

During these early proceedings, Michael was furiously writing notes for John, a practice encouraged by the lead counsel who provided pen and paper for his client. That paid off for Michael, who recognized many within the jury pool; those he thought would vote for and against him.

The jury pool was finally turned over to the individual attorneys. The District Attorney went first.

"Good morning, gentlemen. *Black's Law Dictionary* defines voir dire with the phrase, 'to speak the truth.' It is the only time in which I may speak with each of you. To ask you truthfully certain necessary questions. These questions will help me and defense counsel to determine who can serve as unbiased jurors who will render a just verdict."

He then called each potential juror to the stand and asked if they heard about the case through newspaper or television. Each said, "Yes." The publicity of the case had spread through three Southern states. The prosecutor then asked if that publicity helped them to form any preconceived notions concerning guilt or innocence. The District Attorney then went down the list of standard questions concerning possible dealings with law enforcement, acting as witnesses in prior trials, and most importantly, if any had ever served as prior jurors in a criminal case, and if so, what was the verdict in that case. The prosecutor ended with the all-important query about the death penalty.

"As a juror, if you find the defendant guilty of murder, can you vote for the death penalty?"

The jury pool was then turned over to defense counsel. The list of questions posed by the defense was similar to the District Attorney's. There were exceptions. John emphasized the State must prove guilt beyond a reasonable doubt. He emphasized it was the State's duty to prove the defendant's guilt, not the defense's.

"Remember, the defendant is presumed innocent until and if it's proven beyond a reasonable doubt that the defendant is guilty."

Next, counsel delved into the personal history of possible jurors.

"Have you been the victim of a violent crime? Has any member of your family been a victim of a violent crime? If so, what was the crime? What was the outcome?"

If the answer was "yes," there might be a basis for eliminating a person as a juror. The individual would be released "for cause." That would take place during the actual selection of a jury.

When voir dire was completed, the jury pool was released for forty minutes. During that time, the attorneys, along with the Judge, started to pick a jury. Michael remained in the Courtroom, along with the Court reporter. By the end of the first day, only three jurors were selected. All three were white and male.

The next day the entire process began again. By lunchtime, a jury was selected. Recess was called for lunch and with trial proceedings began again at one-thirty that afternoon. It was time for opening statements. The District Attorney was first up. This proved to be nerve-wracking for Michael. The District Attorney went through three possible outcomes, pursuant to a verdict.

"First, you as the jurors could find the defendant guilty as charged, in which case he would be sent to the gas chamber for the murder of Lois Ferriday last June 22. Or he could be found guilty with the recommendation of life imprisonment. You as jurors could find him guilty and not be able to agree on punishment, in which case it would be an automatic sentence of life imprisonment. You as jurors could find him guilty and not be able to agree on punishment, in which case it would be an automatic sentence of life imprisonment. Third, the defendant could be found not guilty by reason of insanity. The judge would then be required to send the defendant to the State Mental Institution at Whitfield, Mississippi. If you find him not guilty because of insanity, yet of sound mind now, then the defendant could walk out of the Courtroom a free man."

After a brief pause, the District Attorney continued, "Gentlemen, I'm now going to tell you why you need to find this young man guilty as charged and send him to the gas chamber. The evidence presented in this case will prove that this young man killed his grandmother with unimaginable brutality; that he literally destroyed her body with a pipe and two guns – a pistol and a shotgun; and that he left the home he shared with that sweet lady in shambles."

As he highlighted the witnesses, the State would call and the evidence that would be produced, Michael's pulse began to race. His face became devoid of color.

CHAPTER ELEVEN

fter the District Attorney completed his opening statement, attorneys for the defense proceeded to present their statements. John Mason was first.

"Good afternoon gentlemen. I realize after listening to the District Attorney's grab bag of horrors, it's hard for you to have any sympathy for my client. I ask that you keep an open mind. Please keep an open mind when you hear the testimony of Michael's mother, and what her son was exposed to as a young child. Listen carefully to the testimony of his maternal grandmother, as she shares Michael's anguish, and his hurt. Michael Ferriday was a lost boy who was a product of his past."

The attorney continued to lay out Michael's defense and explained why the jury should find him not guilty by reason of insanity. Once he completed his forty-minute statement, Jeffrey Bennett, as co-counsel, presented his theory of the case.

After opening statements, the Court took a short break. Michael felt better. His attorneys were eloquent and forceful. He felt he had some hope for the future. He smiled at the end of the day, as the guards took him back to his cell. But no one saw his smile and he didn't smile again until everything was over.

Once the break was completed, the State began its case-in-chief. An early witness was Emma Jenkins, Lois Ferriday's cook. She walked slowly up the aisle to the front of the Courtroom, her knees weakening with each step. As Emma approached the witness chair, she felt her heart would pound out of her chest — she didn't dare look at the twelve individuals sitting in the jury box for fear she would lose her nerve and run from the Courtroom. As she raised her right hand and swore to tell the truth, she glanced at the jury for the first time. It unnerved her to think twelve white men would be listening to her testimony, judging what she had to say.

After giving her name and address, Emma stated she had worked for the victim for a number of years. She explained Michael hadn't lived with his grandmother for very long. When the District Attorney asked about the afternoon of June 22nd, her voice began to quake. For several seconds, no one could hear her as she softly made her reply. The District Attorney, losing patience, insisted she raise her voice above a whisper.

"The Court reporter can't hear you. It's necessary for you to speak louder. I'll ask you again. What time did you arrive at the home place?"

"Five-thirty. I always arrived at five-thirty to cook supper," she replied, as she looked warily toward the jury box.

"What, if anything, makes you so sure it was five-thirty?"

"I had my watch on."

The prosecutor, in a demanding tone, then asked the frightened cook what happened next.

"As I approached the home, I heard squawking and shouting. I knew it was Michael. There was the sound of someone beating or hammering something. I ran up the steps to the front door and looked in."

"And what did you see?"

"It was horrible. I saw Mrs. Ferriday's body all broken up and bloody. Her face was beat-in." At that, the poor cook hung her head and began to weep.

"After you viewed the body, what did you do?" asked the District Attorney, as he looked in the direction of the jury to see their reaction.

"I ran across the highway to the General Store. The owner called the Sheriff for me. I waited there until the Sheriff came," she responded, as the tears now ran freely down her dark cheeks.

"And did you tell the Sheriff what you had heard and seen?"

"Yes sir." She was visibly shaking at this point.

"You said you heard squawking and shouting, is that right?" The District Attorney continued questioning the cook, refusing to acknowledge her heightened emotional state.

"Yes."

"What if anything made you think it was Michael doing the shouting?"

"I knew his voice. I heard him scream like that before," she answered, still shaking as she lowered her head, refusing to look the District Attorney in the eyes.

"When he didn't get his way?" the District Attorney asked, looking in the direction of the jury.

"Objection!" John shouted.

"Sustained." The judge motioned for the District Attorney to continue.

Looking somewhat smug, the District Attorney turned to address Emma. "Tell us about Michael and his grandmother. Were they close?'

"At times they were. At other times, no."

"What do you mean?"

"They fought – disagreed over the girl. Mrs. Ferriday wanted him to break it off."

"Why?" The District Attorney pushed the cook, trying to drive his point home.

"She felt he was too young to get serious. I agreed and told him so. Said he needed to get an education before marrying."

"How did he take being told no?" Asked the District Attorney, again trying to drive his point home to the jury.

"Not well. He would get real upset."

"Rather spoiled, wasn't he?"

"Objection!"

"Overruled"

After a lengthy direct of the Negro cook, the State turned the witness over to the Defense.

"I tender the witness."

John smiled as he walked across the Courtroom. He stood right in front of Emma on the witness stand and to the left of the seated jurors; close enough to reach out and touch them. He looked at Emma and got right to the point.

"His behavior wasn't like other boys his age was it?"

"No sir." The defense counsel's reassuring smile helped to calm the cook's frazzled nerves.

"When he threw a fit, he would fall out on the floor and convulse wouldn't he?"

"I don't understand, sir?" The cook had a confused look on her face.

The defense counsel rephrased his question to her. "He would fall on the floor and shake all over wouldn't he?"

"Yes sir. He sure did. It was scary," she replied, shaking her head at the memory of his fits.

Looking down at his notes, the defense counsel asked, "he sometimes stared out into space, didn't he?"

"Yes sir." This time she answered in a more confident tone. Her expression and voice grew a bit calmer.

"And he talked to himself, right?" Counsel again looked at the cook, gazing into her eyes to help keep her on track as she sat up straight in her chair, knowing that she was answering the questions correctly.

"Yes, sir."

"He did that after his fits, didn't he?"

The cook nodded in agreement. "Yes, sir, quite a bit."

"So his behavior was not normal, according to you."

"Objection! The witness is not a psychiatrist. She can't testify as to what is or isn't normal," the District Attorney loudly protested as he jumped to his feet.

"Your honor, she can give her opinion, based upon her life experiences," responded John, protesting in an equally loud voice as he jumped to his feet.

"Overruled!" responded the judge.

The defense counsel took a deep breath before asking, "Did he ever tell you that he had conversations with the Lord?"

"Sometimes," Emma said, nodding her head.

"Who else did he tell that to?" The defense counsel questioned her, trying to make his point with the jury.

"His grandmother."

"Did this concern her?"

"Yes sir. She told me she was at her wit's end," Emma said in an empathetic voice. For the first time, she turned and looked directly at the jury box.

After completing his cross examination, John turned the witness over to Jeffrey, who then asked Emma questions about the last two weeks before the murder. He established that Michael's relationship with his grandmother deteriorated during those last weeks. The State was then given an opportunity to correct any damage done by the defense in cross-examination. It was called re-direct. It was a futile attempt.

CHAPTER TWELVE

The State called the Sheriff and his deputies to testify. After establishing his name and position, the District Attorney asked the Sheriff to tell the Court what occurred on the afternoon of June 22, 1957. Lumbering to the front, the Sheriff paused, looking directly at the jury box to see who he might recognize.

"I got a call from the owner of a convenience store on Highway 3," he said confidently.

"That out in the county?"

"Yes sir, near Satartia."

"What happened next?" inquired the District Attorney.

The Sheriff looked directly at the jurors and answered in a louder-than-necessary voice. "I interviewed the family cook. It was hard. She was hysterical, poor thing."

"And what did she tell you?"

He responded, still looking directly at the jury, almost as if he were daring them to disbelieve him. "Well, she told me about the squawking and shouting she heard."

The prosecutor looked down at his notes before asking, "And what else?"

"She said she rushed up the steps to the front door. That's when she saw the mutilated body of Lois Ferriday."

There was a loud communal gasp from the audience. The judge hammered his gavel and demanded silence. He looked at the District Attorney and nodded for him to continue.

"After you got her statement, what happened?"

"I went to the house myself, with my two deputies."

"Once you arrived at the house, what occurred?"

The Sheriff glared angrily towards the defendant as he spit out his words. "We went inside the house. It was awful. As long as I live, I will never forget it."

"Please continue, Sheriff," prompted the District Attorney.

"Well, the first thing I saw was Mrs. Ferriday's body. It was in the hallway."

The District Attorney began to move slowly toward the jury box while addressing the Sheriff. "Please, describe what you saw."

The Sheriff hesitated, taking a deep breath and letting it out slowly. "Her face was shredded, unrecognizable. She was nude and it appeared that she had been shot several times. The lower half of her body was lacerated. I almost threw up, and I have seen a lot." There was another audible gasp from the audience. Some of the men shook their heads in disgust, while others looked sick.

"Were photographs taken at the scene?"

"Yes, of the body and the house, which was in shambles," responded the Sheriff, never taking his eyes off the jury.

"After viewing the body, what did you do next?"

"We went throughout the house taking pictures and collecting evidence. There was blood in every room, starting with the victim's bedroom. It appeared Michael dragged the body through each room in the house." The

Sheriff noticed that the jurors were all looking at Michael with expressions of disgust on their faces. Michael looked down, not returning their gaze.

"What else did you observe?"

"Every bit of furniture was either smashed against the wall or on the floor."

"Where had this occurred?"

"Literally everywhere in the house. Every dish, every bit of the China was destroyed. The television was kicked in. The refrigerator, which was rather large, was turned over and every mirror in the house was shattered. Even the telephone was destroyed." Several spectators looked in the direction of Michael's mother, Lisa, who had tears flowing down her lovely face.

"After you took pictures, what did you do next?"

"We collected evidence. We found the bloody pipe, the pistol and the shotgun he used to kill his grandmother." A loud murmur spread among the spectators. The judge raised his gavel once more to quiet the crowd.

The District Attorney leaned in toward the Sheriff and asked, "Anything else?"

"We found Mrs. Ferriday's ring and money among Michael's bloody clothes. Obviously, he was planning to run away, escape before he passed out in a drunken stupor."

At that point, the District Attorney glanced at the jury and smiled. "Did he mention how much he had to drink?"

"Yes, a half a pint of whiskey and four beers."

"Enough to cause a drunken rage?" inserted the District Attorney, now smiling broadly.

"Objection!" The defense counsel screamed as he hopped to his feet.

"Overruled."

The District Attorney, without missing a beat, asked the Sheriff, "Where did you find Michael?"

"Passed out in the front bedroom, nude. It was the only room he hadn't destroyed. The description of Michael's physical condition caused several members of the jury to look at one another questioningly.

The Sheriff's deputies testified they threw a blanket over Michael's nude body and forced him to look at the broken body of his grandmother before they put him into the cruiser. They told the Court how Michael howled, yelling that he wanted to die, and to kill him on the spot.

After their testimonies were complete, all pictures and objects confiscated were marked and introduced into evidence. The pictures were in color and very graphic. Seeing them had a dramatic effect on the jurors. Several winced and looked away. Others became dizzy, their faces drained of color.

Just then, a spectator in the crowded Courtroom fainted. The judge, along with others, rushed to the man on the floor to help. He was revived and given water.

"Are you alright, sir?" asked the judge.

"Yes, your Honor. At least I was this morning when I consumed two vodkas for breakfast!"

The man was quickly rushed from the Courtroom. This unnerving phenomenon repeated itself. Later that afternoon, another spectator fainted. After that, the judge called it a day. The Court concluded its proceedings. The judge told those involved that the Court would begin the following morning promptly at nine o'clock. He also informed the crowd that he expected all spectators to remain respectful-- and sober -- while in the Courtroom.

CHAPTER THIRTEEN

The following morning the trial started with a jolt. The prosecution began with the doctor who had examined the body of Lois Ferriday, as well as examining Michael just three hours after the murder. After the doctor gave his name and listed his medical accomplishments, the prosecutor asked if he examined the victim's body.

"Yes, and I took notes of my examination. I have a type-written transcript of those notes."

"Referring to your notes, what was the condition of the body?"

"She had been shot four times, twice with a pistol and twice with a shotgun. There were gunshot wounds to the heart, stomach and intestines," responded the witness.

Members of the jury winced. There was no response from the audience other than looking down or glancing at Michael.

"Was that the cause of death?"

"Yes, but there were other injuries as well."

"Please, continue."

"Her face was beaten with a pistol. Serious damage was done to the facial area. Every bone was broken. The lower half of her body was lacerated, and she suffered from blunt-force trauma. It was, if I may say so, overkill."

"Doctor, she was found nude, as was the Defendant. Was she raped?"

"I don't believe so, but the lower part of her body was mutilated." Lisa and Carol looked at each other, the pain showing on their faces. Lisa began quietly sobbing.

After a lengthy examination and limited cross, the doctor's transcript was admitted into evidence. But before the prosecutor was through with his questions, he asked the doctor if he had also examined Michael.

"Did you examine the Defendant at any time?"

"Yes. I examined him three hours after his grandmother's death."

"And what did that involve?" The jurors leaned forward as the doctor discussed the medical examination of Michael.

"I took blood, his temperature, and checked his heart rate and blood pressure."

"And what were the results?"

"Everything was normal - his vitals, for a seventeen-year-old, were perfect. There were no drugs in his system."

"What else did you observe?" The District Attorney leaned into the doctor as he asked his questions, wanting more from his witness.

"I could smell liquor on him. Also, there were scratches on both arms. His grandmother probably fought hard for her life."

There were visibly angry looks on the faces of many of the jurors.

"Anything else?"

"Yes, he admitted to killing her."

By this time, the defense counsel was frowning, and the co-counsel looked to the jury for their reaction.

"What exactly did he say?"

"He said, 'I'm not afraid to die. Go ahead and kill me. Nobody loves me but God. I did wrong and I'm ready to be punished. I've never been happy in my life. I killed someone.'"

Many in the Courtroom were staring intently at Michael, who never raised his head.

"And what did you say?"

"I asked him who he killed."

"What did he say?"

"He said 'I killed my grandmother.'"

The District Attorney shook his head and sighed loudly, as if in disapproval. "Did he tell you how much he had to drink?"

"Yes, he said he drank half a pint of whiskey and four beers."

On cross, defense counsel asked the doctor if the defendant's demeanor appeared normal.

"No. The things he said to me did not appear normal," the doctor stated.

"What did he say or do that appeared abnormal?" The defense counsel asked while looking back at his client.

"Objection! The doctor is not a psychiatrist," yelled John, jumping to his feet.

"Your Honor, he can give his opinion based upon his experiences, as a family physician," explained the defense counsel as he walked toward the bench.

"Overruled."

Smiling, John walked back to his witness and asked, "Again, doctor, what about Michael's behavior appeared abnormal to you?"

"The fact that he wanted to die. That he said no one loved him. That he had never been happy. That is not a normal or healthy response."

"Anything else?"

"He had a wild look on his face. He was shaking and crying, as well."

"Doctor, have you examined him, since?

"Yes, shortly after a razor was found in his jail cell."

"What was the purpose of that visit?"

"To make sure he hadn't injured himself and to determine if his mental state required a suicide watch," explained the physician, looking again at his notes to be sure he didn't leave anything out.

"And did it?"

"Yes. He was glum, listless, and unresponsive. I felt he needed to be watched."

After releasing the doctor from the bench, a short recess was called.

The next two witnesses to take the stand were a couple from Satartia. They were neighbors of Lois Ferriday's. They testified to seeing Michael on the day of the murder. After swearing in each witness and obtaining names and addresses, the prosecutor asked the couple where they were late on the afternoon of June 22, 1957.

The husband answered, "I was driving us home on Highway 3. Suddenly, I noticed the defendant driving erratically, right before he passed me," the witness answered in a confident manner, looking directly into the faces of the jury.

"What do you mean, 'he was driving erratically?'" The District Attorney was standing close to the witness while the defense took notes.

"Well sir, he was all over the road, swerving back and forth," answered the witness, never taking his eyes off the jury.

"Anything else?" The Defense Attorney walked back to his table to retrieve some of his notes.

"Yes. He scared me to death. He was driving thirty miles an hour before suddenly accelerating to sixty-five miles an hour. That was right before he passed me. I told my wife he was probably drunk."

The District Attorney looked at his notes and wrote something on a legal pad. He then looked up and asked the witness, "At what time did that occur?"

"I'm not sure of the exact time. It was somewhere between 5:15 and 5:30pm."

The wife was asked if that's what she observed. She said yes. Her testimony was basically the same as her husband's.

Next to testify were two of Michael's aunts. They said their nephew appeared normal. Both stated he had never exhibited erratic or bizarre behavior. They claimed he was a typical teenager. On cross-examination, John brought out the fact that they were not around him on a daily basis – their infrequent visits with the defendant were not enough to form valid opinions concerning his behavior or his mental state at the time of the murder. The later testimony of Lois Ferriday's niece did offset the cross-examination of the aunts. The niece emphasized the frequency of her visit with the defendant. She stated that she saw Michael every day after school. She said he was a sane, typical, average teenager.

John asked the witness if she saw the defendant on the day of the murder. "No, I did not," stated the witness, emphasizing each word as she stared at John. The angry look on her face said volumes.

"So, you can't testify as to his mental state on the day that your aunt died, can you?" John raised his voice and pointed his finger at the witness before continuing. "You weren't with him twenty-four hours a day, were you? Or even seven hours a day?" He stared intently at the witness, waiting for her response.

"No, sir," she said meekly.

"You were not privy to the arguments between your aunt and the defendant, were you?"

"No, sir." She glared at the defense counsel.

"So how can you say with any certainty that the defendant was sane at the time?" The attorney again raised his voice for emphasis.

"I know what I observed every day after school," the niece responded, her words loud, but clipped. After she was dismissed, she stormed away in a huff, turning to give one last angry stare at John on her way out of the courtroom.

Next, the prosecutor called the jailer to the stand. He told the Court that Michael claimed the food in the jail tasted like poison. He said Michael accused the jailer of poisoning him.

The witness said that in his opinion the defendant was mean but definitely sane."

The last of the witnesses called by the State included the Superintendent of Education and the principal of the high school. Both testified as to the defendant's school activities, intellectual ability, and sanity. The examination of the school principal began with Michael's school activities.

"Did the defendant participate in sports?"

The principal, who was also the former coach, known as "Hard Rock," looked directly at Michael and said "Yes. He played football for three years and baseball for four years."

"What other activities was he involved in?" The prosecutor asked while looking at the school documents placed on the podium.

In the well-moderated voice of a teacher, the principal looked directly at the District Attorney and answered, "he was on the school paper staff, a member of Student Government, Boys' Chorus, Homeroom President, and Junior Rotarian."

Looking back at his notes, the prosecutor asked, "What awards did he receive?"

The principal responded that the defendant qualified for a Gooch Foundation scholarship and alternative appointment to West Point Academy for the 1958 school year. He was looking at the jury as he responded to the District Attorney.

"What about intelligence level?" asked the District Attorney, smiling at his witness, as if to encourage him.

"Above average intelligence and ability in school."

"What about his early high school years?" The prosecutor seemed to be drawing out his witness as he looked in the direction of the jury to determine their reaction.

"He wasn't always studious," the principal stated. "Not until his junior year. Before that, he was a discipline problem. He would cut up in class. Everything changed in his junior year. He got serious about his future after that."

"What about his sanity?" Once again the prosecutor looked directly at the jury as he asked the witness the question.

"Normal. The defendant always appeared and acted normal."

The Superintendent of Education gave essentially the same testimony. He went over the results of Michael's aptitude tests and the last four years of his grades. The witness concluded by saying the Defendant was above average intelligence and appeared sane.

The prosecution's case-in-chief was finished. It was time for the defense to present their case. At that point, the Court declared a recess until the following morning. When he saw the look on Michael's face, it was obvious to John that he needed to meet with the teenager in his cell.

When John arrived at the jail, Michael was sitting in the corner, his Bible on his lap and a look of sheer terror on his face. Michael's skin was drained of color and his eyes were like two black holes. When the teenager looked up John could see the tears in his eyes. There was hopelessness and resignation along with fear in the contours of his young face.

"Am I going to die?" Michael asked. The attorney gave a weak smile and attempted to reassure his client.

"Son don't give up yet. We have excellent witnesses and I'm going to fight hard on your behalf. Read your Bible and pray. But please don't give in to your fears, okay?"

The teenager gave a half-hearted reply. "Yes sir. I'll try."

As the conversation between the two continued, Michael wanted to know what would happen if he survived. "What then? Will I spend the rest of my life in an insane asylum?"

"I hope not, son, although I understand that Whitfield is an excellent facility. It is a self-contained hospital with its own cafeteria, laundry, and numerous other amenities. I've heard good things about their large medical staff. It's not medical abuse or horror stories. According to the doctors I've talked with, Whitfield uses family and individual therapy and the latest medications to treat mental disorders."

Somewhat mollified, Michael gave a weak "thank you" to his counselor. John left the jail with concern for his client. All he could do was fight hard for Michael. His work was difficult at best.

CHAPTER FOURTEEN

Before being called to testify, the defense witnesses sat in an anti-room with one large window, a long wooden table, and a number of wooden chairs. In the corner were stacks of dusty law books, at least twenty years old. Each of the witnesses sat nervously twitching in their chairs. Only the two psychiatrists were calm.

The first witness for the defense was the Presbyterian minister, whom Michael attempted to visit on the day of the murder.

"Please tell us what happened the afternoon of June 22, 1957," John asked.

The minister responded, "I had left the office to run a few errands and when I came back, I found the wall mirror and the thermostat in my office smashed to pieces."

"Continue," urged John.

Shaking his head in disbelief, the minister answered, "It was like someone had ripped them off the wall and thrown them on the floor."

"How long were you gone?" asked John, who was trying to establish a clear timeline for the day.

"Only about an hour or so. When I returned, I noticed the penciled note on my desk." He looked at the attorney in anticipation of what was to come next.

John asked the minister to read the note into the record. As the minister read the contents of the note out loud, John gazed at the jury. Looks of sadness and shock registered on their faces.

Counsel then asked, "After you read the note, what did you do?"

"Two things. I called the police, then I tried to call Michael's home. All I got was a busy signal. I figured he had taken it off the hook. It was later that I discovered he had destroyed it."

"Why did you call the police?"

"I was afraid he may have attempted suicide. I asked the police to do a thorough search of the rectory and the church. It was after that I attempted to call the homeplace," explained the minister, looking in the direction of the jury.

"What conclusion did you draw from the incident?"

"I figured Michael was very disturbed and needed my help, or so I thought at the time."

Standing next to the jury box, John asked, "And now?"

"I still think he's disturbed. I pray for him." The minister lowered his head, as if in prayer before being dismissed from the witness stand.

After the minister was dismissed, Michael's father, Mike, was dismissed from the courtroom before John called Michael's mother to the stand. What occurred next was totally unexpected and rattled the entire courtroom. As she made her way to the witness chair, a blood-curdling scream erupted followed by moans and hissing. It came from Michael, who lost it when he saw his mother. The Sheriff's deputies literally dragged him from the courtroom, as he continued to sob. It took Lisa several minutes to collect herself to the point where she was able to testify. After drinking water, she indicated she was ready. She began by telling how she met Michael's father, about their courtship. The early years of the marriage and the birth of their only child were pleasant enough. But eventually, Mike's drinking got out of hand.

"My husband became a full-blown alcoholic," she stated. "He was drunk more than he was sober, and he was a very mean drunk."

Lead counsel gave her a sympathetic smile and asked, "I know this is difficult, but can you tell the Court what he did to you when he was drunk?"

A frightened look crossed the witness's face, but she continued with her testimony. "He would beat me for no reason. It would start with a slap on the face, then he would punch me. Once he knocked me down, he would kick me hard in the stomach. That resulted in doctor's visits for lacerations, broken bones, and black eyes."

"What did you do, as a result of his violence towards you?"

She began to weep. "I left him and filed for divorce. I knew if I didn't leave I would end up dead."

"How did your son take the divorce?"

"Very badly. He blamed me. He said it had been paradise being with his father, said I spoiled everything and that he's been miserable ever since."

"After the divorce, what happened to your son?"

With a sad look, she responded, often shaking her head in disbelief. "Initially, he lived with me. When he was in the fourth grade, we moved here from Vicksburg. I got a job and my son stayed with me, until his teenage years. After that, he moved in with my mother and later with his paternal grandmother."

"And why was that?

"He was a problem child," she explained as she nervously twisted the ring on her right hand. "As a teenager, he grew hard to handle."

"In what way?"

"He would throw fits, tantrums. Sometimes he would fall out on the floor and convulse. He would claim he was deadly ill when there was no evidence that he was sick." Her eyes began to tear up again, and she reached for a tissue from the box next to the witness chair.

"Anything else?"

"Yes, He would scream at me, claiming I didn't love him. He said he had visions and saw things. He would break things when he was upset. It got worse, the older he got," she said, her voice shaking. Her face registered the pain she felt.

The defense attorney walked to the witness stand and leaned into Michael's mother. He quietly asked, "Please tell the Court what happened on June 22, 1957."

The mother took a deep breath to try to collect herself. She hesitated a moment before speaking. "It was mid-afternoon when I received a number of calls from my son. It was obvious he was agitated, upset about something."

"Continue," encouraged the defense counsel.

"He shrieked into the phone that I may be his mother, but I didn't love him. Even though I asked him several times, he wouldn't tell me where he was. He later arrived at my mother's house on Dunn Avenue.

"How did he appear?" John gave her an encouraging smile.

"Extremely upset. He complained to my mother and I of being sick. That no one cared for him and that he was miserable, saying his life was hell. It was obvious he had been drinking. He was unsteady and we could smell the liquor on him – we didn't want him to leave. If only we had called the authorities to get him help…but we didn't. A little over an hour later, we were told about the death of his other grandmother."

As she spoke, the prosecutor shook his head in disbelief and smiled, occasionally looking at the jury for their reaction. His co-counsel was furiously taking notes.

After the mother's testimony, the judge called for a short recess. Michael, who had calmed down after his outburst in the Courtroom earlier, was brought back in to sit next to his attorney. When the Court reconvened, his maternal grandmother was asked to take the stand.

Lisa's testimony was reinforced by the statements of her mother. Carol said she had seen little of her grandson since he moved to the county in 1956. She was shocked by his appearance and bizarre behavior.

"He was severely disturbed the afternoon of June 22nd," the grandmother stated. "He was unbalanced and not able to understand right from wrong. I thought of telling the police, and I know now I should have."

"What else did you notice?" asked John.

"He was overly anxious about his health, which was not normal. I'm sorry I didn't call someone." She looked in the direction of her grandson. Carol's eyes registered the sadness she was feeling.

"Anything else that you may have observed?"

"Yes, my grandson frequently had tantrums with convulsions and wild facial expressions, sometimes for no reason. He daydreams to excess and frequently complains that no one loves him. He blames my daughter for the divorce." As she wrapped up her testimony, Carol's eyes filled with tears.

"What about since then?"

She visibly calmed herself, then explained, "I have visited my grandson daily since June 22nd. He tells me of hearing voices and conversations with the Lord. He told me the Lord said he was either going to die or inherit a lot of money from a Mr. Alexander in Texas."

"Has he exhibited any other strange behavior?" asked John.

"He's suspicious of everyone. He thinks the jailer is poisoning him."

Throughout her testimony, her grandson refused to make eye contact and kept his head lowered. It has been a full and emotional day, with spectators fainting and even throwing up, not to mention Michael's unnerving reaction to his mother. Everyone was exhausted. The judge called a recess until the following morning.

CHAPTER FIFTEEN

The morning began with the testimony of the chief psychiatrist of the University Hospital in Jackson, Mississippi. John asked the psychiatrist if he examined the defendant and if so, how many times.

"I met with the defendant on three different occasions," said the witness. "He was thoroughly examined, and I was able to make a diagnosis." He answered confidently, looking into the eyes of the jurors as he spoke.

"What was his diagnosis doctor?" asked defense counsel.

Looking down at his notes, the psychiatrist responded, "he met all points in the classic definition of schizophrenia."

"Will you please tell us what those definitions are?"

"Delusions, which are false beliefs not based upon reality. This included delusions of persecution and paranoia. Hallucinations, which involve hearing voices or seeing things that don't exist, along with suicidal thoughts

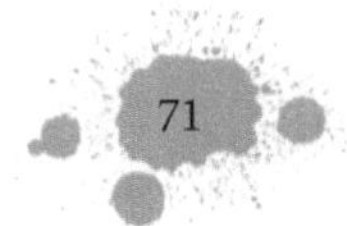

and behaviors are just some of the symptoms, as well as disorganized thinking or speech. He fit the criteria."

"What about the ability to tell right from wrong?"

The witness's response was firm and clear. "No, the defendant is not able to tell right from wrong."

"What about aggressive behavior?"

"Yes, but it's rare. I would be remiss if I didn't mention that alcohol can intensify these symptoms," answered the psychiatrist, emphasizing his words when necessary. It had its desired effect.

"Can it cause the disorder to develop?" As the defense attorney asked the questions of the psychiatrist, the jury leaned forward to better hear the answers.

"No, there's no indication of that."

"At what age would this disorder manifest itself?"

"Schizophrenia would reach its overt state between late teens, early twenties to thirty."

"What causes a disorder like schizophrenia, doctor?" At this point, the jury was hanging on the doctor's every word.

"We in the mental health community are not sure. We believe it may be a culmination of biological and environmental factors. While there is no known cause of schizophrenia, there are genetic, psychological, and social factors thought to play a role in the development of this chronic disorder," explained the witness, who was still looking at the jurors.

"What about exposure to violence, early childhood trauma?"

"Yes," he nodded his head in agreement. "That could be a factor."

"Can this disorder be faked?"

"No, there is no possibility whatsoever of a fake." The doctor emphasized his answer, speaking loudly and firmly.

"Doctor, based upon your knowledge and examination of the defendant, what is his prognosis?"

"Michael needs medical care and has reached the state in his mental disorder that his prognosis is poor even with treatment. Without treatment, it is hopeless." Again, the witness looked directly at the jury, answering with a sense of conviction and hope that they understood what he was saying.

On cross-examination, the prosecution brought up the fact that the psychiatrist gave the defense attorneys a copy of a book on clinical psychiatry that listed the symptoms of schizophrenia. The witness agreed that he did so.

"Yes, I did that. But we received the book only three days before the trial. Certainly, not enough time for the defendant to study it and learn to fake the symptoms listed in the book."

The last witness called by the defense was the psychiatrist from New Orleans. He was a respected professor at Tulane, considered to be a forensic expert. Lead counsel asked the witness if he had examined Michael, and if so, how many times.

"Yes, I met with the defendant several times. The examination of the patient was very thorough, and I was able to render a diagnosis," explained the psychiatrist, not reacting to the noises coming from the direction of the prosecutor.

"And what was his diagnosis?"

"Paranoid schizophrenia."

"Is this a chronic disorder?"

"Yes," responded the witness. "There is no cure."

"And how has this disorder manifested itself in the defendant?"

Looking down at the medical records he brought with him, the psychiatrist carefully gave his answer in detail. "He had delusions of persecution. He constantly said no one loved him. He accused the jailer of poisoning him. There were audio hallucinations - a key symptom of his disorder. He said the Lord talked to him. He said that God told him he would either die or inherit fabulous riches from a man in Texas."

"Were there other symptoms?" John probed.

"Yes, he had the ability to love a thing one minute and hate it the next. He had hypochondriacal attitudes and sexual maladjustments going back to elementary school, where he exposed himself to females. He is still obsessed with the idea of sex," responded the witness, taking a moment to look directly at the men in the jury.

"In his mental state, could he distinguish right from wrong?" asked John.

"No, he couldn't. Nor was he able to understand the severity of his actions."

"At what age does this disorder become active?"

"It takes years for the disorder to reach the overt stage. Most males develop symptoms in their late teens or early twenties which is what happened with the defendant. At the age of seventeen, the disorder manifested itself in the defendant, resulting in the death of his grandmother."

"Could the defendant be pretending to be sick, to avoid the gas chamber?" asked John, driving his point home to the jurors. The question was designed to answer what was surely on the minds of the jurors.

"No, absolutely not. He was not malingering or faking his symptoms. Due to the length of time in which I had the opportunity to observe him, I was able to determine he was suffering from paranoid schizophrenia," said the psychiatrist, emphasizing each word of his diagnosis, never taking his eyes off members of the jury.

On cross-examination, the District Attorney attacked the doctor's credibility.

"Doctor, you're a hired gun aren't you?"

"No, I have expertise in the area of forensic science, which enables me to testify often."

"You spend more time on the stand than I do in Court, don't you," demanded the prosecutor, getting in the doctor's face in an attempt to intimidate him.

"That's not true sir," the doctor defiantly responded.

On redirect, the defense counsel brought out the psychiatrist's numerous credentials for the jury in an attempt to establish the doctor as a valuable expert. That was the reason for his many appearances in Court.

Once both sides had rested, the defense asked for a directed verdict, claiming the State had failed to prove his client was insane at the time he killed his grandmother. The judge denied the motion. The jury was given a recess and the courtroom emptied. The process of establishing what jury instructions would be given to the jurors began in earnest. Both sides submitted their instructions, subject to objections by either side. Ultimately, the judge decided which instructions would be given based solely on present case law. Once this was completed, the jury was called back to the courtroom. The judge read out loud the instructions. They were then given copies of the submitted instructions.

It was time for both sides to give their closing arguments. It was the last chance for the prosecution and defense to convince the jury to accept their version of events. As the Judge pointed out, closing arguments were not evidence. A jury must decide guilt or innocence based on the evidence itself. But it was an opportunity for each side to tie up loose ends and present their theory of the case in a clear, concise, and believable manner.

CHAPTER SIXTEEN

On the third day of the trial, the courtroom was overflowing with people. Everyone wanted to hear the closing arguments. Razor-edged tension filled the air. Both sides realized it was their last chance to convince the jury of the defendant's guilt or innocence, and both sides felt strongly about Michael's sanity.

While he normally ate a big breakfast, John Mason was doing well to consume two cups of coffee that morning. Neither the District Attorney nor Jeffrey Bennett were very hungry either. The Defendant was nauseous. The crowds, on the other hand, were excited. They knew the attorneys representing the defendant were admired for their brilliance in the courtroom. Besides local folk, the District Court was filled with members of the press from as far away as Memphis and as distant as New Orleans.

Lead-counsel entered an anteroom and said a quick prayer. Many years later, he told his daughter that any lawyer who didn't get nervous before trial wasn't worth his or her salt. That same nervousness would keep

lawyers at the top of their game, but the nerves had to go away once they opened their mouths to speak.

After the Court was called to order, the judge read jury instructions. "Members of the jury, you have heard all the testimony in this case. What I am stating to you from this point on is the law that applies to this case. It is my duty to instruct you as to the law and it is your duty as jurors to follow these instructions."

The judge went on to instruct, "Regardless of any opinion you may have as to what the law ought to be, it would be a violation of your sworn duty to base your verdict upon any other view of the law than that given to you in these instructions. Your oath as a juror requires you to follow and apply the law. Regardless of any opinion you may have about what the law should be you must, under oath, follow these laws in reaching your verdict."

"You must decide what the facts are in this case. In other words, you must decide what happened. In making these decisions, you are expected to use good judgment and common sense." After what seemed an eternity to read the comprehensive instructions to the jury, the judge concluded with, "The attorneys will now make closing arguments. These arguments are intended to help you understand the evidence and apply the law. But the arguments are not evidence. Therefore, if a statement is made during the arguments which is not based upon evidence, you should disregard the statement entirely." The judge had reminded them that all twelve of the jurors must agree on a verdict before they can return it into open Court as the verdict of the jury.

The State got two bites at the apple. The prosecution went first, followed by the defense. And the State got one more chance to present their side in a final argument.

Brandishing the half pint of whiskey found in the ruins of the ten-room house, the District Attorney shouted, "Here's a buck and a half worth of schizophrenia! The defendant wasn't insane. He was enraged. Someone told him no! His grandmother." Waving the whiskey bottle in the faces of the jurors, the prosecutor continued with his tirade.

"You've heard the testimony of numerous witnesses. You've seen pictures of what the defendant in a drunken rage did to his grandmother – he shot her, pistol-whipped her, lacerated her, mutilated her, and left her home in shambles. You've seen the weapons he used to destroy his grandmother. Gentlemen, you've heard the testimony of his aunts and his cousin, who spent every afternoon with the defendant. That same cousin who said Michael was sane. You heard the testimony of his high school principal and Superintendent of Education, who testified that he appeared sane and had above-average intelligence. Intelligent enough to fake the symptoms of schizophrenia. There's the testimony of the jailor, who was in close proximity to the defendant for months, who said he was not insane, just mean. This young man who was a spoiled only child, who threw tantrums to get his way. A young man, who was not used to being told no."

The prosecutor continued in the same vein, "So when his grandmother wanted him to break off a relationship, what did he do? He murdered her, in an awful, brutal, and horrible way. The poor woman fought for her life, as evidenced by what the doctor said about the scratches on the defendant's arm. And how do we know he was faking his insanity? Let's look at his letter to his minister trying to create sympathy for what he was about to do."

Taking a moment to let the jurors soak in his words, the prosecutor continued. "If the defendant didn't know right from wrong, why did he take his grandmother's ring and money from her? All of which were found among his bloody clothes. The defendant was planning to escape before he passed out in a drunken stupor. Why attempt to escape if the defendant didn't know he had done wrong and was trying to escape the consequences of his actions?"

The District Attorney again paused, this time taking a hard look in the direction of the defendant before continuing. "Now gentlemen, let's look at the hired gun, who testified on behalf of the defense. The psychiatrists were paid well for their testimony. In fact, one of them has been on the stand longer than I've been in front of the Court. So, who do you believe, the testimony of those who have been around the defendant a lot longer than those who hired guns, including his aunts, his cousin, his educators, and the jailor who guarded him for the last five months? Who do you believe, gentlemen?! I ask you to find the defendant guilty and punish him for his foul deed."

With that, the District Attorney thanked the jurors for their service and glared at Michael before returning to his seat.

John sighed and shook his head. He walked up to the podium and looked into the faces of jurors. He took a long moment before saying a word.

"Gentlemen, what you have just heard is fantasy. The young man you see at the defense table is not mean. He is sick. This young man suffers from paranoid schizophrenia. Yes, you heard the testimony of his aunts, his cousin, his educators, and the jailor. None of them were as close as those who lived with him, who raised him. His mother and maternal grandmother both testified to his mental disorder. None of the State's witnesses had a real long-term relationship with Michael, other than his cousin. But his cousin only saw him after school and was not alone with him. She did not live with him nor raise him. She did not visit him in jail on a daily basis. She did not see him on the afternoon of June 22nd. She did not witness his pain or his long-term anguish. This boy's disorder is a product of his environment, particularly his early years when he witnessed his alcoholic father viciously beat his mother. The trauma of that helped to bring on the disorder he suffers from now."

John paused slightly before continuing. "The District Attorney accused the psychiatrists who testified of being 'hired guns.' Yet both doctors are very distinguished and knowledgeable experts in forensic medicine. That's why they have testified in many Court cases. Remember their credentials that were brought out under sworn testimony. These experts told you that it is impossible for this young man to fake schizophrenia. A disorder this complex and multi-faceted cannot be faked."

Looking again into the faces of the jurors, John continued his closing statement. "Gentlemen, the defendant had no real motive for the terrible deed he committed. It was an insane act, one not caused by drunkenness. You've heard the chief psychiatrist at University Medical and the forensic expert from New Orleans, who both testified that Michael's prognosis is poor with treatment, and without treatment, it's hopeless. Do not send this young man to the Parchman Penitentiary. He has a mental disorder. He needs help instead of punishment. Please bring back a verdict of not guilty by reason of insanity. Put him in a maximum-security cell in Whitfield, where even a cockroach can't escape."

John continued in his heartfelt plea for another twenty minutes before turning the jurors over to Jeffrey, who addressed the District Attorney's accusations. "The District Attorney claimed the defense framed this case by giving the defendant a textbook that sets forth the symptoms of schizophrenia. This was supposedly done so the defendant could fake a mental disorder. Remember, both psychiatrists stated there was no possibility of the disease being malingered." John stood up and reread the youth's farewell note to his minister and quoted the line, 'God is punishing me.'"

Jeffrey continued. "It's symbolic of mental disorder when the words are compared with what the youth told his family physician soon after the crime, that God had forgiven him." He ended by reminding the jurors of the law.

"The law says the State has to prove beyond a reasonable doubt that the defendant was legally sane at the time of the murder. Otherwise, you must find Michael not guilty by reason of insanity. Jeffrey paused briefly and continued.

"If the State is unable to prove this, you must find Michael not guilty by reason of insanity. The law states the insane should not be punished for what they do. Remember the testimony of the psychiatrist who said the defendant needs medical care, even though he's not likely to get well. And remember, the doctor stated that Michael's chances were poor, with treatment, and hopeless without."

Jeffrey ended with a plea. "Do not send the defendant to Parchman because you will be adding to the tragedy by putting Michael where the doctor says it is hopeless."

CHAPTER SEVENTEEN

Next came the County's Attorney, who was assisting the District Attorney. It was his turn to convince the jury of the defendant's guilt. He began by telling the jurors that the "sexual atrocity" committed by the defendant was the most heinous crime ever to take place in the County. "The doctor who examined the victim couldn't say she was raped. But the evidence certainly indicated the hideous perversion to which she was subjected."

The County Attorney continued with his condemnation of the defendant. "This young man is feigning the symptoms of paranoid schizophrenic. He read the books given to him by the defense and faked the disorder. He is simply a stubborn hard-headed youth, who didn't want anyone to tell him what to do. You need to find him guilty so that he will not be allowed to prey on society ever again. What this young man did was not insane, but an evil act." Pointing a finger at the Defendant, the Attorney said, "He admitted to killing his grandmother because she wanted him to break off a relationship. For this reason, he slaughtered her. Gentlemen, he is sane, and he needs to be punished for what he did, and not admitted to Whitfield. Come back with a just verdict, a verdict for the grandmother he brutally murdered."

After the County Attorney completed his closing arguments, the jury retired to come up with a verdict. It was 5:35 p.m. on Saturday afternoon. The judge recessed the Court. The Defendant sat in his wooden chair staring glumly at the floor. The District Attorney went back to his office to return phone calls. Jeffrey called home to say he would be late for supper. Understanding, his wife agreed to put up a plate for him. Michael's mother sat in the corner of the courtroom, talking privately with her mother.

Across the room, sat the father of Michael. When John returned to the courtroom, Mike rushed over to Michael's attorneys to ask what his chances were. Both told Mike they had no idea.

"No one knows what a jury will do until they do it," said Jeffrey. Both attorneys went downstairs to get a soft drink from the machine and to smoke another cigarette.

Waiting was the worst part for everyone, but it was especially difficult for the attorneys. They had done everything possible to present a winning case. Now it was out of their control. All they could do was pray and wonder what the verdict would be. Would the jury find Michael guilty without a recommendation, which meant the gas chamber, or would he spend the rest of his life in prison? They couldn't help but wonder what Michael was thinking and feeling. They wondered about his mother and maternal grandmother, talking quietly in the corner of the courtroom.

Both sides felt sorry for the women. It was a tragedy for all concerned, no matter what the verdict. The townsfolk, along with the press, waited patiently outside of the courtroom. No one wanted to guess the outcome. It had been an emotionally draining case for those who loved Lois Ferriday, as well as for those who loved Michael. The youth of the town and county were also affected by the trial. Their innocence was forever damaged. It was now the end of the 1950s, with the 1960s on the horizon. Maybe the case was an omen for things to come. The loss of innocence, a more violent society. A town where people would eventually lock their doors and look over their shoulders.

All that would come later. Many who knew Michael would go on to college, get degrees, and settle into their careers. Many would marry and begin the process of raising a family. But none would forget what happened on Saturday, June 22, 1957, or the three-day trial that came later.

After nearly an hour, Lisa and the Carol could wait no longer. They thanked the Defense Attorneys and asked them to inform them of the verdict as soon as possible. Carol spoke briefly with Michael before leaving the courtroom. Finally, at 7:03 p.m., the twelve-man jury brought back a verdict. Within minutes, the District Court was packed, with all looking in the direction of the jury room. Once the judge was seated on the bench and the jurors were seated, the judge asked the foreman to hand over the verdict. The Circuit Clerk read it out loud.

"We, the jury, find the defendant not guilty on the grounds of insanity." They certified that Michael was dangerous and had not been restored to reason. When the verdict was read there was total silence. No one cried out, no one commented, no one said a thing. Michael, who had sat expressionless throughout the trial, suddenly smiled.

The judge thanked the jurors and dismissed them. The room was emptied of spectators and members of the press. Michael and his father thanked his attorneys for what they had done. Both sides shook hands. The Circuit Court Judge signed an order immediately committing Michael Ferriday to the state mental hospital at Whitfield, Mississippi. Before being transferred, Michael and his father posed for pictures in the court anteroom.

The local paper's headline read: "Defendant acquitted, Judged Insane and Dangerous. Trial Ends with his Commitment."

It took the Sheriff's department close to an hour and a half to transport Michael to his new residence. John Mason and Jeffrey Bennett went home to their families for a late supper. The press hurried to available phones to call in the verdict. The family of the victim, the great aunts, and the cousin were left to absorb the outcome of the nightmare that began four months before.

As Michael traveled to Whitfield, he became uneasy. He had heard stories, frightening stories. He prayed they weren't true. As the Sheriff's transport pulled into the front gates, Michael marveled at how lovely the grounds were.

Michael's life was full of twists and turns. His stay at Whitfield included many things. It was full of torment, realizations and even healing. It eventually led to his redemption and release.

Michael's family sold the murder house and the land it was built on. The house no longer stands as it once did. It slowly began to deteriorate from lack of use. Neither Michael nor his immediate family ever came back to the town.

John Mason went on to try another murder case, but none as infamous as the 1957 case. Months after the trial, he was asked to run for Governor. He gave it some consideration and turned down the offer. He loved politics but from a distance. His daughter was disappointed. She felt he would have made an excellent Governor. His wife and older children were relieved.

CHAPTER EIGHTEEN

Mississippi State Hospital for the Insane was located at Whitfield, Mississippi. It was named in honor of Governor Henry L. Whitfield. Constructed on a former convict farm, the hospital was located eight miles east of the state capital. The facility was opened on March 4, 1935. The main hospital and adjacent buildings covered three hundred and fifty acres with buildings in the Mount Vernon style. A lake was created in front of the main buildings. The hospital was self-sufficient with its own bakery, dairy, laundry, and well for water. In addition, there was a beauty parlor, printing facility, and sewing shop. The grounds were beautiful with sweeping green areas and stately oak trees. It was more like a wealthy estate than a prison or hospital for the insane.

In 1935, three thousand patients were housed at Whitfield. They were segregated by race. Each racial group had its own chapel, dining area, and recreational facilities. Patients were also separated according to age, violence, intelligence, and tuberculosis. By 1950, there were over four thousand patients. By 1958, the year Michael Ferriday was found not guilty by reason of insanity for the killing of Lois Ferriday, there were four thousand and five hundred patients with ten psychiatrists, eighteen physicians, and twelve consulting physicians.

The Superintendent of Whitfield at the time genuinely cared for the patients. He was instrumental in changing the hospital into something beyond a prison atmosphere. Michael was actually lucky to be a patient at that time in the hospital's history. Psychiatrists were beginning to rely more on medicine along with therapy, and less on more extreme methods of treatment. However, doctors in the late 1950s still favored artificial fever therapy and electroshock therapy. At that time, mental patients were not put to sleep during electroshock treatment but instead suffered from painful and frightening experiences. This was something Michael would be subjected to.

Upon arrival, Michale, who was now eighteen years old, was taken to the locked-down forensic unit. His first impression was that he had exchanged one prison cell for another. His first night was a sleepless one. He wondered if his life at Whitfield would be any better than a life of imprisonment at Parchman Penitentiary.

The next few weeks involved the diagnostic process. Its purpose was to rule out other mental disorders and to determine if the symptoms Michael suffered from were not influenced or due to substance abuse, medication, or another medical condition. He was given a thorough physical examination that included drawing blood, peeing into a cup, checking his pulse and heart rate, as well as more intimate prodding. The process took almost a week to complete.

By the end of each day, Michael was exhausted. Once the procedures were completed and he was given a clean bill of health, Michael was subjected to a different set of tests designed to help rule out other conditions that were similar to schizophrenia. There was also screening for alcohol and drugs.

The most thorough, timely, and extensive evaluation for the new mental patient came next. The psychiatric procedures included meeting with the Chief Psychiatrist at University Medical. His notes from interviewing Michael on three separate occasions while he was incarcerated were reviewed by doctors at Whitfield. Michael's mental status was checked by health professionals at the hospital. The doctors observed the patient's appearance and demeanor. Michael was asked about his thoughts, moods, delusions, hallucinations, past substance use, potential for violence and suicide. His family and personal histories were discussed in detail, with an emphasis on early childhood. His feelings for his father and mother were examined. The most painful part of his evaluation was the inquiries about his grandmother. Early talks resulted in hysterical episodes in which Michael was sedated and taken back to the forensic unit.

Once the diagnostic process was completed, a treatment plan was created. He received electroshock treatment on a weekly basis and talk therapy on a daily basis along with medication. His treatment plan included individual therapy and later, family therapy.

As time passed, Michael began to look forward to individual therapy. His feeling of anticipation didn't extend to electroshock treatments. It was something Michael never got used to. He started writing letters to John Mason, the young attorney who had represented him at trial. It was a habit that he continued throughout his life. The attorney appreciated the letters from his former client. The Chief Psychiatrist at University Medical kept John up to date on Michael's progress. The attorney looked forward to the letters and monthly updates. He began to hope for Michael's continued improvement and maybe, just maybe, his eventual release.

People in town began to forget about Michael. He was locked up, and they went on with their busy lives. As long as he was at Whitfield they were safe. Most didn't want to think of him ever again.

His parents reacted differently to his incarceration. Michael Ferriday Sr. didn't live in town so public scrutiny didn't bother him. As long as he could get his hands on his whiskey he was content. Lisa Ferriday moved away, back to Belzoni, as did her mother. Their feelings for Michael were mixed and very painful. Despite what he screamed at her; the mother loved her son. She wanted to see him, but his doctors felt it was too soon. Michael needed to examine his anger toward her as well as his grief over the absence of his father, and his sense of abandonment. She knew she had to deal with her other feelings toward her son. He reminded her of her former husband. She feared the violence in both of them.

And there was the girl he had loved. What she felt now was horror and shame. She feared people would know she was the one who had loved and been loved by a monster who slaughtered his grandmother. Michael never saw her again and she was glad. She had to live with her regrets, and she had many of them. If only she had recognized the demons in him before it was too late. Unlike Michael, she didn't seek the benefit of therapy. She cried herself to sleep most nights and was often awakened by vivid nightmares.

The notoriety of the case faded into the back pages of old newspapers. There were other cases, and other events to capture the imaginations of the public. Television took over the former role of the newspaper to keep the public informed. Television elected a young president, illustrated the thrill of space travel, and kept the country on the edge of their seats during the Cuban missile crisis.

CHAPTER NINETEEN

Michael settled into the routine of everyday life at Whitfield. It gave him a sense of security, and with that new confidence he was able to begin to explore the feelings that led to the killing of his grandmother. As the guard released him from his cell and escorted him to his counselor's office, Michael smiled. He took in the colors and smells of early spring. He had been at Whitfield for five months. He didn't want to be there forever. But for now, it felt like home, albeit a temporary home.

He smiled again at the psychiatrist as he entered the doctor's office and sat down. He was asked the standard questions.

"How are you feeling today?"

"Calm," Michael responded. "Calm and focused. No voices. Just enjoying nature."

"Excellent, what about your earlier suspicions?"

"Nothing really. But I still have negative feelings about my mother."

"Do you want to talk about that?"

"Not yet. I want to talk about my memory. Why can't I remember what I did to my grandmother?"

"There are several reasons for that. Electroshock therapy causes temporary memory loss, and you didn't remember before those treatments. I believe it's your way of protecting yourself from what you aren't ready to handle. Also, there's the alcoholic blackout. You may or may not ever remember. How are you feeling about what happened?"

"Same as before. I feel grief and shame at what I did. I don't understand my rage. When I think of the girl I love that feeling is fading. I can't really remember what she looks like. It's just a vague image now."

"So you don't love her?"

"Not with the same intensity. Not with the same fear of losing her."

"So there were feelings of abandonment?"

"Yes, I think it goes back to my father."

"I think you're right," said the counselor. Michael nodded in agreement. "Let's explore those feelings shall we?"

"I feel alone without the comfort of love. I feel lost and I can't find my way to happiness. I haven't felt really happy since my parents divorced. No, I take that back. I was happy playing football."

"Were you close to your coaches?"

"Yes, I was."

"Maybe they were substitute fathers for you. They filled the hole your father left."

"Maybe, yes."

When the session ended Michael was escorted back to his cell. He surprised himself by not thinking about his feelings of abandonment, but instead about what he was going to eat for supper. He hoped his meal was either pork chops or fried shrimp. That's what he requested. He was tired of meatloaf.

The next year's treatment continued in an established routine. Michael gradually stopped hearing voices. His anxiety lessened. He began to understand his fears of abandonment. He developed a knowledge of his parents' marriage, and why his mother had to escape the abuse. His letter writing increased to include his mother and his maternal grandmother.

He looked forward to their letters, as well as his attorney's type-written responses.

His therapist decided it was time to expand his sessions to include family therapy. The first of the sessions was with his father. It didn't go well, resulting in a full-fledged argument over the father's excessive drinking. Michael wanted his father to get help. His father grew angry and lashed out.

"Boy, I don't have to take this," the father said, raising his voice. As he stood up and prepared to leave, he said, "You've got a lot of nerve, considering how I stood by you after you killed my mother!"

"Daddy, I'm not trying to judge you," Michael responded. "I just want you to get help, to live a long life." Michael reached out and touched his father's shoulder. "I'm sorry, Daddy."

The father removed Michael's hand and stalked out of the room. Future sessions didn't improve over time. The visits and attempted breakthroughs grew less and less. Michael quickly realized he couldn't talk openly with his father the way he did with his therapist. The male support he wanted wouldn't come from his father.

His meetings with the mother and grandmother were more successful. Their relationships were not without some torment on both sides. Michael's previous outbursts at his mother had taken their toll. She was hurt and wary of him, even scared of him. He still felt pain over his mother's supposed rejection. It was hard to understand why she had asked others to take on the responsibility of dealing with him. If she was his mother and truly loved him, why did she reject him? Those were issues they would work through together over many visits and many therapy sessions. All took place with the guidance and presence of the therapist. As time passed, Lisa grew less wary and more comfortable with her son. Michael became more affectionate towards her. He started to care for her and she cared for him.

Michael and his grandmother Carol had already established a caring relationship while he was in jail. During their visits, she updated him on the people in his hometown. He was interested in his prior attorneys and their families. He was glad to hear about the children of his former advocates; that they were doing well and making plans for the future.

She told Michael that best friend growing up had recently started classes at Ole Miss. Michael asked Carol about the girl, the one Michael had once loved. She said there wasn't much to tell.

"She moved away, and her family is pretty close-mouthed about where she went."

"I hope she finds happiness."

"Do you plan on seeking her out at some point?"

"No," said Michael. "She's part of my past. I need to leave her alone. I've caused her enough trouble."

Suddenly he reached out and hugged his grandmother and kissed her on the cheek. Deeply moved, she squeezed his hands.

"I'm so glad to see you like you are now," she said. He laughed and said, "Me too!"

As time passed, he eagerly looked forward to their visits and counted the days in between. Another welcomed change was that his psychiatrists changed his electroshock therapy and went from weekly sessions to once a month. He was given cafeteria privileges and more freedom. He enjoyed his daily walks around the grounds. He spent much of his time at the pond, watching the birds landing in the water.

CHAPTER TWENTY

s Michael entered the dining hall, he noticed a child not more than fifteen sitting alone in the center of the room. He decided to say hello to the kid. He shook Michael's hand and told him his name. The boy mumbled his name and looked down at his plate.

Three years into his commitment at Whitfield, the patient had become a young man. Michael was given more freedom, and he had frequent visits with his mother and grandmother. His father's visits were almost non-existent, usually only during Christmas or Easter, but very little in between.

The young man had cafeteria privileges and enjoyed most of what was offered at the hospital. He enjoyed long walks on the lush grounds. He spent time beside the man-made lake. Whenever his grandmother would visit, they would spend time together at the lake. He loved their quiet time together. They discussed the young man's future, rather than his past. After three years, the patient, along with his mother and grandmother, hoped for his eventual release. They discussed where he would attend college, what he would major in, and what kind of career he hoped to have.

The future was also the topic of conversation the young man had with his therapist. He told of meeting the teenage boy in the cafeteria, and that the boy obviously needed help.

"Maybe that's my future vocation, to work with troubled youth." The therapist asked about the meeting. "It was at the dining hall. I noticed him sitting alone in the center of the room. I went over to say hello, and he reminded me so much of myself three years ago.

"In what way?"

"Well, the kid's head was down. He looked at his plate and barely spoke."

"The same way you did during your trial," reminded the therapist.

"Correct. He told me he was at Whitfield for wrecking a classroom. He also broke into a store and stole beer and cigarettes."

"What makes you think you can help him?" asked the doctor.

"I think he is suffering from the same fear and anxiety I was plagued with."

"You're not a psychiatrist," the therapist reminded the young man.

"I know, but maybe I can help him to talk. I could encourage him to see the help that's available here."

"Just as long as you don't neglect yourself. Yours is a life-long fight against the effects of schizophrenia."

"I understand," said the young man. "I realize it's something I will have to deal with the rest of my life."

As time passed, Michael began to request books from the hospital library that dealt with adolescent psychology and psychology in general. He wanted to know what type of courses he needed to take in order to get a degree in psychology. He was also interested in juvenile justice. He wanted to know how to apply to law school and receive a degree from various jurisdictions, including Georgia, Texas, and Mississippi.

His doctor advised him to slow down and take it one step at a time. He also emphasized the need to concentrate on his ongoing treatment. "You don't need to lose sight of your disorder. What you need to do is to remain stabilized. Don't take on more than you should at this point in your treatment."

Michael laughed. "Doctor, you sound like my grandmother. She is always cautioning me to take it slow."

"She is a wise woman." The doctor continued along the same vein. "Don't get grandiose in your thinking. Remember your past belief, that you would inherit millions and live a grand lifestyle."

"Yes, I remember. I just want to work with young people," Michael insisted.

"That's fine. But right now let's work on your mental health, shall we?"

Michael's medical team was concerned that their patient was under the delusion that he was cured – something he would never be. He could control his disorder with medication and weekly therapy sessions. If needed, hospitalization and electroshock therapies would be available. But he would never be free of the unfortunate disorder that once led to tragedy.

With the advent of the 1960's, new drugs were available and there was less reliance on other methods of treatment. Michael was given medication that didn't make him drowsy. He was fortunate not to suffer side effects from the new medications. His treatment team continued his weekly therapy sessions, which sometimes included his mother and/or grandmother.

Eventually, the time came to consider Michael's release. When he was first admitted, no one, not even Michael, had contemplated a possible release. To consider the release of a patient diagnosed as a paranoid schizophrenic within three years was unthinkable. His treatment team knew it would be an uphill battle. There were the people in power that had to be considered. A committee of psychiatrists and attorneys would have the final vote on his release from Whitfield.

Michael's team would have to convince the committee that the patient was ready for release. They had to present their papers consisting of medical records, therapy notes, and all other results of various treatments for consideration. All documentation would have to show steady proof of continued improvement. Progress needed to be illustrated in his records, along with his doctors' observations. All were considered during an extensive question and answer session.

Next, the committee would need to interview Michael before voting on his release. The treatment team spent the last six months of 1960 preparing for their presentation before the committee. It also gave the team more time to determine his fitness for release. Michael was eager to prove he was mentally ready. He was subjected to verbal and written tests. His team incorporated the results into their final notes, which went into documentation for the committee.

Finally, the team needed to talk with the man's mother and grandmother. His doctors needed to hear what they thought. Did they think Michael was ready for the world outside of Whitfield?

CHAPTER TWENTY-ONE

(December 1960)

The day for the committee meeting finally came. Michael was up early and got dressed quickly before going straight to the dining hall. He woofed down a plate of scrambled eggs and toast before rushing to the chapel and saying a prayer for a positive outcome. He took long strides across the grounds as he walked to his therapist's office. The young man was eager to talk to his doctor about the day's upcoming events. As his doctor ushered him into his cluttered office, covered with files and a desk piled high with various documents, the young man smiled and asked, "What do you think Doc? What are my chances?"

The doctor looked up from his notes and responded, "I think they're pretty good. But I don't like to guess. Let's just concentrate on putting our best foot forward."

"Sure, any last-minute instructions?" asked the young man.

"No. Let's go, we don't want to be late."

The doctor patted his patient's shoulder and led him out of the office. The two men headed toward the building where the committee would meet. The meeting room consisted of metal folding chairs, a podium, and a long wooden table at the front of the room. The young man was asked to wait outside the meeting room with an orderly until the committee was ready for him.

He sat in a hallway on a bench and watched as a Special Assistant Attorney General from the Attorney General's Office passed by him, along with two lawyers who were in-house counsel for the Department of Mental Health. They were followed by a slew of psychiatrists and board members who also entered the meeting room.

After everyone was seated, various members of the committee were introduced, along with in-house counsel and the Special Assistant Attorney General. A member of Michael's medical team walked to the podium and introduced himself. He began by reviewing the patient's history.

"The patient was arrested on June 22, 1957, for the murder of his paternal grandmother. She was shot four times, with a pistol and shotgun, and beaten with a pipe, which was also used to leave the ten-room house in shambles. It was overkill, which is, of course, common in patricide – the murder of parents and grandparents. Law Enforcement found the mutilated body of the grandmother in the hallway. She was nude. The seventeen-year-old was found in the front bedroom, also nude except for his socks. At the time of his arrest and during his trial, the patient exhibited many of the symptoms of paranoid schizophrenia. He heard voices. He was delusional and very paranoid. During the trial, the patient was removed from the courtroom screaming, moaning, and hissing, when his mother took the stand. The chief psychiatrist from the University of Mississippi Medical Center and a forensic expert from Tulane University in New Orleans, Louisiana, testified that the boy was paranoid schizophrenic. They both predicted a poor prognosis for improvement. The psychiatrist from Tulane University stated that the patient suffered from hypochondriacal attitudes and sexual maladjustments. After a three-day trial, the teenager was found guilty by reason of insanity and committed to this hospital. Please review the typewritten notes, pursuant to the patient's history and early treatments, copies of which are being passed out to you, along with a list of medications the patient was given."

One of the committee members asked why the poor prognosis.

"According to the testimony of the forensic expert, the schizophrenia had reached the overt stage."

Another committee member asked what the prescribed treatment was for the patient and what tests were given when the patient first arrived at Whitfield.

"He was given a thorough physical checkup. After that, he was tested for intellectual capacity and then a mental evaluation was done."

"His prescribed treatment?

"Sorry, yes, it's fully set out in your copies of his mental teams' notes. The patient was subjected to electroshock treatments, given anti-psychotic medications, and daily therapy sessions with various psychiatrists on the treatment team.

"What was the team's early prognosis?" asked another committee member.

"Poor. However, it should be noted that there was some disagreement as to the patient's diagnosis. Some individuals on the team felt the teenager had been misdiagnosed. That the patient had a psychotic break or a result of some trauma he had suffered.

"And now?"

"There's still some disagreement, but all agree his present prognosis is excellent. He has responded unusually well to treatment."

The question-and-answer session continued. Later documents on the patient's treatment were passed out to committee members. This went on for several hours and ended with discussions of medication for the patient, upon his release from the hospital.

"He will be given prescriptions of appropriate medication, along with addresses for the mental health facilities existing within the state. The patient will receive contact information of various medical professionals who specialize in dealing with his disorder."

Once his review with his team was completed, Michael was ushered into the meeting room. After he gave the committee his name, age, and other personal information, he was asked,

"Do you understand the purpose of this interview?"

"Yes, to determine if I am mentally ready for release."

"And do you believe you are cured?" asked another Whitfield physician.

"No, I know I have a chronic disorder -- one that can be stabilized with medication and therapy. But my condition can never be cured."

Next, the committee members had an opportunity to ask specific questions relating to the patient's past symptoms.

"Do you hear voices?"

"No."

"Do you think others are out to hurt you?"

"No."

"Are you suffering from an incurable disease, such as cancer?"

"No."

After extensive questioning was conducted, the committee asked about the patient's future.

"Tell us about your plans, if you are released from State Hospital."

"I want to apply and enroll in college."

"Where will you apply?"

"Mississippi State University, for sure. I may also apply out of state, to Alabama and maybe the University of Texas."

"And what do you plan to do once you graduate from college?'

"I'm hoping to work with troubled youth. I may even further my training with another degree. I'm not really sure at this time. My doctors have urged me to take one step at a time. I'm trying to follow their advice."

After the interview was over, the young man was asked to wait in the hallway. The committee took a vote and agreed to grant his release.

CHAPTER TWENTY-TWO

(1961)

The thought of being released from the protective cocoon of State Hospital proved to be daunting for Michael Ferriday. Where would he stay before enrolling in college? Which college? He had no money for tuition or clothes. He would have to depend on his grandmother and mother for assistance. Fortunately, they had already thought about those things, setting aside money for college. They found relatives for him to live with until it was time to leave for school. (Why wouldn't they let him live with them? And why did he go to Vicksburg – where his dad lived? Why not with them?) They picked him up at Whitfield and drove him to Vicksburg. His gratitude was immense. He didn't think he could ever express it adequately. The guilt, however, was still with him and would always be there.

On the ride to Vicksburg, he rolled down the window and took in the sights and smells of the winter season. It was hard to believe he was finally free to live his life. This time he was without hate, without fear, without delusion.

Michael had spent very little time in the town by the river. His father lived there but didn't raise Michael. The young man fell in love with Vicksburg. He liked the rolling hills, the Mississippi River and the brick streets that still graced downtown.

The downtown was teeming with businesses. Main Street was lined with women's dress shops, men's haberdasheries, and many other shops of all kinds. Then there were the restaurants. The Old Southern Tea Room was Michael's favorite. Lena would drive over to eat with Michael on Sundays. He always ordered the plantation chicken, which was fried and then steamed. His side dishes were corn casserole and bread pudding, followed by lemon cake with custard sauce.

The history of Vicksburg intrigued him. He spent hours in the Vicksburg Military Park, wondering how Union troops got those huge cannons up the steep hills. He visited the Vicksburg Museum and toured McRaven, an antebellum home said to be haunted. In the months before college, the young man never ran out of things to do.

While he longed to return to the town where he grew up, his relatives warned against it. The townsfolk had not forgotten the murder, nor the trial that followed. When he wasn't busy exploring Vicksburg, the young man worked on his admission forms for Mississippi State. He thought about leaving Mississippi, but he wasn't ready to be that far from home.

He took his medication and found a doctor in Jackson that he visited twice weekly. He didn't attempt to date anyone. He knew it was too soon. He knew he didn't need to complicate his recovery with a romantic relationship, although the man did wonder about his former girlfriend. He hoped she was well and happy.

The last week he spent in Vicksburg was spent shopping for, and later packing, his travel trunk with numerous items. It included his socks, underwear, belts, shirts, pants, sweaters, and coats. He packed everything he could ever use or wear while attending Mississippi State.

The man's final week in Vicksburg was bittersweet. He was leaving the river town he had come to love. At the same time, he was looking forward to the next chapter of his young life. This was his chance to learn, to educate himself and to obtain a degree. After that, who knows what challenges he would take on. He knew he couldn't wait to find out. He also knew he would come back to the river town, but he would never live there again. As his mother drove him toward his new destination, he rolled down the window and took in the sights and smells of the drive. He felt he had a new lease on life, and he was ready to make a good future for himself.

The town of Starkville was nestled in the eastern part of the state. It was close to the Alabama border, an easy drive to Tuscaloosa. That fact would take on later significance. The University was renowned for its School of Veterinary Medicine. The young man's major was quite different. His interest was in humanities, not science. After he settled in his dormitory, he took a tour of the school. There were red brick buildings scattered throughout the large campus. A nice-sized football stadium was part of the mix. His first day on campus ended in the cafeteria where he consumed his supper, although the food was not as good as what he had enjoyed at Whitfield. The young man laughed to himself and thought a college cafeteria was still preferable to a mental hospital.

As he lay in his new bed in one of the men's dormitories, he wondered about registration. Would he run into people he knew? He wondered how they would react. He soon found out. There were catcalls, vulgar language, and death threats. It made him sick to his stomach. He grabbed the list given to him at State Hospital and rushed to the nearest pay phone. He made an appointment with a local psychiatrist near campus. Several hours later, he entered the doctor's office. He gave the physician his history and details of his treatment at Whitfield. He told the therapist what happened at registration.

"How did you feel?" asked the doctor as he wrote in his notebook.

"Horrible," responded the young man. "Sick to my stomach."

"Did it surprise you?"

"No, I guess knew it was coming. But it still bothered me."

The doctor stopped writing, gazed at the young man, and said, "You will either need to transfer to another college or learn to deal with the insults because they won't go away."

The blunt words of the doctor shocked him. But he knew in his heart that his therapist was right. There was nothing he could do to stop the insults. He had to learn to live with them. The physician interrupted the man's thoughts and said, "Just don't respond. Look straight ahead. Pretend you don't hear them. It's the best thing you can do to keep the abuse from escalating. If you complain you will make it worse."

"Thank you, doctor. I have no intention of complaining," said the young man as he rose to leave. On his way out, he made another appointment with the receptionist.

The next day classes started. The young man concentrated on his courses which helped him forget about the early abuse. It all came back with an incident in the library. He was sitting at a table working on a homework assignment when he looked up and noticed a group of students sitting at the far end of the library. They were staring. It was not anger he noticed, but fear. Several of the young men looked pale. There was pure terror in their eyes. They all got up quickly and practically ran out of the library. That hurt more than the anger. They were terrified of him. He wished he could assure these young men that he had no intention of hurting them. But he knew it was useless. He was aware that there were many at the University who knew who he was and what he had done. He knew those individuals would react with either anger or sheer terror.

CHAPTER TWENTY-THREE

The feeling of isolation was intense for Michael. He now knew what it was like to be shunned. The angry outbursts were replaced by other students who gave him a wide berth. He sat alone in the cafeteria. In the classroom, no one would sit near him. Every seat in front of him, behind him, to the left and right of him was empty. He made no friends on campus. While others were attending fraternity parties and going to football games, the young man sat alone in his dormitory room. He had no roommate.

All he did was go from his dorm room to the classroom and to the library. He looked forward to his weekly therapy sessions, more for the human contact than anything else. The only bright spot was that his grades were excellent. The library was his second home. He asked his relatives for help in purchasing a secondhand vehicle. It gave him a sense of freedom. He was free to escape the isolation and the hate that seemed to surround him.

Michael had to be careful when he went. There were student hangouts in and around Starkville he had to avoid. He didn't go to nearby Columbus. All the females at the Mississippi State College for Women (MSCW) had been warned against him. Off-campus boyfriends and students from his hometown made sure the girls at the "W" knew about Michael Ferriday. They were warned to stay away from him, for their own safety.

He drove further and further away from the State campus. On the weekends, he traveled east, crossing the Mississippi-Alabama line. Finally, one weekend Michael drove all the way to the University of Alabama. He traveled through the campus and marveled at how beautiful the grounds were. He parked his automobile and walked miles through the grounds, exploring the campus. It became a weekend ritual for him.

He noticed female students throughout the campus. His first attempts at meeting co-eds were disasters. Despite his good looks, he was awkward, tongue-tied, and because of his awkwardness, maybe even a little scary.

Michael had grown into a handsome young man. He had dark hair large penetrating brown eyes, and pale skin. His full lips centered his face. He was average weight with broad shoulders. He was a bit self-conscious about his height -- he was only five feet, eight inches. His short stature, however, did now stop girls from giving him the once-over.

It had been a long time since he had talked to girls his own age. Michael had almost given up when the young man spotted a lovely slender coed leaving the library. Her arms were full of books. When she dropped her load, he rushed over to help her. She smiled and thanked him as he kneeled to pick up the numerous books she had been carrying. He introduced himself and offered to carry the books back to her dormitory. She told him her name was Janice Dove, and as they walked, she told him she came from a small town in Alabama. She was a junior and working on a term paper. "Hence, the reason for so many books," she said. "Are you a student here?" she asked.

"No, I go to Mississippi State," he responded.

"Oh," she said, wondering what he was doing in Tuscaloosa.

"I got bored and decided to take a road trip."

"Oh, I see." She picked up her step toward her destination. She thanked him and rushed into her dormitory. He realized he had scared her. But he wasn't ready to give up. The young man wanted to see her again. He wanted to assure her he was safe to know.

On the way back to Starkville, he racked his brain trying to figure out how he could approach the pretty coed without frightening her. If only he knew someone who could act as a go-between. But there was no one. He knew he had to approach her slowly, not come on too strong. He couldn't just call and ask her out. He concluded that a chance meeting would work out best.

His opportunity came several weekends later. Janice was at a student hangout, right off campus. She was there with her roommate and several other friends. They accidentally bumped into each other. He smiled and said, "We meet again! No books I see."

She smiled back and asked if he wanted to join her and her friends. He charmed the group by sharing some limited information about himself. He told the girls he was from a small town in the Mississippi Delta, and that he played football and baseball in high school. He mentioned his major and that he wanted to work with juveniles once he graduated. He also hinted that he was unattached, but not adverse to meeting someone with whom he could connect. Not everyone was impressed. The girl's roommate was suspicious.

"There is something he's hiding," she told Janice. "I'm sure of it." But Janice already had a crush on the handsome stranger. It started when they shared hamburgers and fries later that day. The young man wasn't so sure. For the sake of his mental health, he wanted to take it slow.

They didn't go out every weekend. He figured every three weeks was enough. They went to the movies or a local diner for hamburgers or fried shrimp. Nothing too romantic, and no alcohol. Janice began pushing for more. He used his studies and exams coming up at the end of the semester as an excuse. He still had three more years of study to complete. On the other hand, she was about to finish her junior year.

Then there was the issue of the murder and the trial afterward. How could he tell Jancie, who thought he was an average college student, that he brutally murdered his grandmother? How could he explain that he was tried for that murder, found insane, and sent to a hospital for the insane? That he remained there for three years? How does he tell her all that and not expect her to run from him screaming? Most girls would run scared. Would she?

There were two people he needed to discuss his fears with -- his mother and his therapist. The doctor advised him to tell the girl before things got serious between them. "What if the two of you decided to date exclusively or get engaged and you wait until then to tell her? It would be traumatic for the young woman to hear such a thing at that point."

"Yes, I see what you mean."

His mother agreed.

"Tell her while she is still not serious about you. Tell her when she can make a clear-headed decision concerning you. You have to be fair with her.

"Yes mama, you're right, but it won't be easy."

When it was time to see Janice again, Michael spent his time driving to Tuscaloosa to think about when he would tell her. But the most difficult issue was what he would tell her. How do you tell a girl you like, who you might get serious about, that you murdered your grandmother?

CHAPTER TWENTY-FOUR

Michael decided to meet Janice on the campus of the University, where they originally met. It was a beautiful Saturday afternoon. A warm sunny day. He found a bench near the library and watched as she walked toward him. She looked especially pretty in her argyle sweater set.

Janice sat down beside him. He leaned over and kissed her on the cheek. She knew immediately that something was off by the look in his eyes. He appeared apprehensive; like someone caught in the act.

"What's wrong?" she asked.

"I've got to tell you something," he responded. "I prefer you hear it from me than someone else."

"It must be something bad."

"It is," he said. He took a deep breath and blurted it out. "Back in 1957, on June 22nd, I killed my grandmother."

"Stop joking. That's not funny!" she responded in an aggravated voice.

"I'm not joking. I shot my grandmother four times. I beat her with a pistol and pipe. Then I destroyed the entire ten room house we lived in. I left it in shambles."

All the color drained from Janice's face. She bent over and let out a wail. She began to sob and scream "no" over and over again. Michael reached out to console her. She pushed his arm away and continued to cry, shaking uncontrollably. It frightened the young man. He wanted to calm her, but he had no idea how to do that. When she finally stopped crying the look in her eyes was a combination of fear, confusion, and pure hate.

He recognized the look. He had seen it so many times. Tears rose in her eyes once again. He tried to speak but nothing came out. She watched him in a detached way. Not saying anything, just looking at him like he was a bug under a microscope.

"Why?" she finally asked.

"I was diagnosed with paranoid schizophrenia and put in the State Hospital for the insane. I was there for three years."

"Good grief!" the girl yelled. "No more, please. I've got to go. We'll talk later."

At that point, she left the bench and ran toward the brick building in front of the dormitories. By the time she reached the dormitory, Janice was sobbing again. She ran to her room and threw herself on her bed. She cried until her eyes were swollen shut. The girl fell into a deep sleep, as a result of shock and exhaustion. Her roommate came in late and didn't bother to wake her.

The next morning Janice told her roommate – her closest friend -- what happened the day before. Nothing could remove the look of shock and horror on her friend's face. "What are you doing to do?"

"I don't know," Janice answered. "This is a nightmare."

"I'll tell you what you ought to do," responded the roommate. "Run like hell!"

"Here I thought I had found the man I wanted to marry. I thought he was perfect in every way! I've had some pretty awful blind dates before, but never anything like this! A homicidal maniac that murdered his poor grandmother. He left her lacerated, bloody body on the hallway floor, then he spent three years in the nut house. And to think I was actually going to take him home to meet my family."

Janice's roommate laughed and said, "I would love to be a fly on the wall for that meeting. Mom, Dad, I want you to meet my intended. He just got out of the nut house for slicing up his grandmother after shooting her four times."

"It's not funny!"

"No, you're right," said the roommate. "It's like something out of *The Twilight Zone.*"

"I know he will want to talk, but I'm not ready yet."

"What are you going to say to him?" asked the roommate.

"I don't know," Janice responded. "I'm still trying to take in that awful confession. It reminds me of Edgar Allen Poe."

"Yes, it's pretty creepy. You've got to get him out of your life. You don't know if he's safe to be around," added the roommate. "Did he tell you he's cured?"

"No. It's a chronic mental disorder."

"Well, there you have it. Stay away from him. Let's go to the cafeteria."

"No, I'm not hungry."

For the next three days, Janice wouldn't eat and she refused to get out of bed. Michael did not attempt to contact her by telephone. He realized he had to give her some space. However, he did send her a letter. In it, he explained about the trial itself; and how he felt about his grandmother. He told the girl of the guilt he felt and the grief that were constant companions. He told her about his medical treatment at Whitfield, which included electroshock treatment. Then he expressed his feelings for her and what he hoped for their future relationship.

"Each day my feelings for you increase. I will never harm you or anyone else, ever again. I take my medication and there's my weekly therapy. I'm a God-fearing man and attend church on a regular basis. I want you to meet my family, especially my mother and maternal grandmother. I'm hoping that we will have a future together. I know you need time, but please remember you mean a great deal to me. I don't want to lose you."

It was everything Janice was hoping for before she knew about Michael's past. She had a lot to consider. She couldn't just write him off as her roommate insisted she do. Her feelings for him were too deep. She decided to make an unusual request. The girl wanted to meet with his therapist.

Michael approached his therapist about Janice's request. He gave his doctor permission to discuss anything that she might want to know about him. His therapist agreed to a one-time meeting with the young woman. Michael offered to drive Janice to the doctor's office. She refused his offer. Instead, her roommate drove her to the therapist's office in Starkville. During the entire trip, her roommate tried to convince the girl to break it off with Michael.

"You understand you're considering a future with a man who was judged dangerous by a jury. A man who spent three years in a hospital for the insane. A paranoid schizophrenic, who's only stable as long as he takes his medication. What if he gets off his medication?" she asked.

That was a question Janice couldn't answer.

CHAPTER TWENTY-FIVE

Janice was rather shy, so meeting with the man's therapist was difficult, at best. Her roommate drove her to Starkville and escorted her into the doctor's office. Michael was waiting when the two of them arrived. After giving him a menacing glare, the roommate left, telling her friend she would be back in an hour.

So unsure of herself, Janice made a list of questions to ask the psychiatrist. After introductions, the therapist asked Michael to wait in the outer office until the interview was complete. He smiled at the reluctant girlfriend and asked, "You have a list?"

"Yes sir. I made a list because I was afraid I would forget what I needed to ask."

"It's okay my dear. I won't bite," he laughed, "What's first on your list?"

"This disorder, schizophrenia, is there a cure?"

"No. I'm afraid not. It can be controlled through proper medication and therapy but there is no cure."

So, he has to stay on the medication forever?"

"Yes."

Doctor, do you think he will stay on his medication?"

The psychiatrist smiled and said, "I'm not a fortune teller, but I do believe that your boyfriend is a safe bet. I think he will remain on his medication."

"But you can't guarantee that, can you doctor?" interrupted Janice.

He answered with a single word, "No."

"Do you think he's dangerous?" she asked.

"Certainly not in his present state. He is safe, stable."

"But if he gets off his medication, what happens then?"

"Based on the symptoms of his disorder and the guilt he carries, it is much more likely that he will harm himself, rather than others."

"Thank you, doctor," the girl replied as she rose from the brown leather chair she occupied.

"Is there anything else?"

"No sir. Thank you." With that, Janice left the doctor's private office and joined Michael. She could tell he wanted to ask her if she was satisfied. He wanted to know if she could give him a chance or break it off. It wasn't an answer she was ready to give. She gave him a sympathetic look and said. "You have to give me time."

Obviously disappointed, he nodded his head and said, "Okay."

On the way back to Tuscaloosa, Janice was deep in thought. She said very little to her roommate. Basically, she repeated what she had told Michael. She needed time to think. The weeks that followed were difficult for both Michael and Janice. He was anxious, worried what she would do. She was conflicted. One minute she wanted to cut her losses and end the relationship. Other times she wanted to take a chance on her new boyfriend. But she was already half in love with Michael.

Janice weighed the pros and cons of each decision. One of her major concerns was her family. How would her parents feel if she continued to date the young man? How would she convince them that he was safe to be around? If she stayed with him, boundaries would need to be set.

Finally, she agreed to meet with him. It was another beautiful day on campus. Michael was waiting for her, seated on the bench near the library.

As Janice approached, she smiled and answered his unspoken question with a "yes." They both agreed to certain ground rules. There would be no drinking, no sex. They would take it slow. They met on the weekends. They continued to go to movies, eat out at the local diner, and went to church together. He had been raised as a Presbyterian. She managed to find a local church with which he was comfortable. He liked the minister, and his sermon didn't conflict with his basic beliefs. This was the path the couple took for the next couple of years. There were no wedding plans. He needed to complete his education at Mississippi State.

Ironically, Michael was on a very different path from the one he wanted to take at age seventeen. There was also the problem of the girl's family. Their objections to the match was strong. Her father threatened to cut her off financially if she didn't end the relationship with Michael. That meant no continued education. The young couple couldn't afford to pay for her college as well as his.

Janice's mother was even more adamant. She told her daughter she would disown her if the girl continued to see the young man. Janice begged her parents to at least meet with him. She asked if she could bring Michael home for a weekend visit. Finally, Janice revealed that Michael had proposed to her. After much begging, crying, and insisting, her parents agreed to meet with the fiancé.

Michael did his best to charm both parents. They were pleasantly surprised with both his charm and manners. They were still cautious and insisted on a family conference near the end of the weekend. The young man agreed to answer any and all questions.

Janice and her parents assembled in the family's den with Michael. A brick fireplace centered the room, and the wood paneling and leather chairs gave the room a cozy feel. Janice's started the questioning.

"What are the symptoms of your disease?"

Looking into the eyes of the father, the young man responded, "It's a disorder, not a disease, and the symptoms can include hallucinations, paranoid behavior, hearing voices, depression."

The mother responded with an equally probing question. "Is your disorder chronic, or is it curable?"

"It's not curable," the young man explained. "But it can be controlled through medicine and therapy. I promise you that I will always adhere to my treatment plan and stay on my medicine and continued therapy."

The questioning ended with the father who asked, "How are we to trust that you are telling us the truth?"

Michael smiled and said, "I spent three years in a mental institution. Do you really think the psychiatrists would have released me if they had any doubt I might be a danger to myself or to others?"

Near the end of his senior year, Michael wrote a letter to his former attorney. He asked his lawyer for a written recommendation – he was going to apply to law school in the State of Georgia. He was accepted, and his fiancé went with him. They found an apartment near campus.

The couple was married at the home of Janice's parents, in a garden ceremony officiated by a minister. It was a pleasantly cool fall day. The rose garden was in full bloom with yellow and white roses. There was a small deck with a wrought iron table and matching chairs. The outdoor furniture was moved and replaced with flower arrangements and a white cloth carpet leading from the patio door to the deck.

It should have been a perfect day for the girl from Alabama, but it was marred by the disapproval of her roommate and the concern of her parents. Her old roommate cornered her the night before the wedding and gave Janice a dire warning.

"If you marry him, it's going to end badly. I can feel it in my bones. I'm not trying to upset you. I'm just scared for you. You may hate me for saying this, but you're my best friend and I want you to be happy. I don't think you can be happy with that man." The girl began to cry, and her roommate broke down as well. It ended with both girls sobbing in each other's arms.

On the day of the wedding, the bride's parents called their daughter into the den and asked her if she was sure she was doing the right thing. Her father asked, "Honey, have you really thought about your future with that boy? What if the guilt he feels becomes too much and he harms himself?"

Her mother interjected at one point and said, "What if he has a breakdown and ends up in another mental institution? What would you do then? And there's the issue of children. What if they have their father's not-so-healthy genes?"

Despite all the warnings and concern, the girl was still determined to be his bride. Late that afternoon, Janice's old college roommate served as her maid of honor, wearing a rose-colored dress. Janice walked down the aisle dressed in her grandmother's wedding gown made of old lace and satin. Janice and Michael were pronounced husband and wife.

The next three years were demanding for the couple. Michael spent most of his time in the law library. He went to classes and spent his free time preparing for class assignments and making outlines on each subject. It was a necessary task if he wanted to pass his exams. Meanwhile, Janice kept the apartment clean, shopped for groceries, and cooked hearty meals for her husband. She had a lot of time on her hands. She missed her family and friends.

After months of loneliness, she found a solution to the empty hours. She tutored college students at a local community college.

They both wanted a family but not at that time. While law school was stressful for the young man, he continued follow his doctor's orders. He stayed on his medication and went to therapy sessions. His young wife joked that she needed the therapy more than he did. There was little time for socializing or date nights. A prime example of his simple-minded devotion to the law was when his wife found him in bed with a law book resting on his chest. Forget sex, forget cuddling.

For the first time in a long time, Michael became friends among his fellow students. It was a relief not being stared at or talked about, and not openly insulted. These new friends knew nothing about his past. All they knew was he was from Mississippi, a good student, and had a sweet, devoted new wife. Despite the stress, those years were some of the happiest times of the young couple's life.

Michael looked forward to giving something back. He still wanted to work with troubled youth. He felt he was uniquely capable of dealing with juveniles. His past history gave him a special understanding of the demons that troubled teenagers faced.

CHAPTER TWENTY-SIX

(Spring 1967)

As his law school education came to an end, Michael had to decide if he wanted to practice law with the attorney he clerked with in college. He still dreamed of counseling young people. Then there was his desire to leave Georgia and move to Texas, something he had dreamed of doing since he was a teenager. He talked things over with Janice, who encouraged him to take chances. She told him not to do what's necessarily expected.

As they prepared to leave their first home to move to Texas, Janice had unexpected news to share. She wasn't sure how her husband would take the sleepless nights and the extra expense. She was thrilled, but would her husband be happy about the new addition to their family?

During the last dinner in their apartment, she broke the news. "I'm going to have a baby!" she exclaimed.

The young man looked startled and asked, "Are you sure?"

"Yes."

"How far along?" he asked.

"Three months, I think. Are you upset?" she questioned, suddenly anxious.

"No, of course not," he assured her. He broke out in a smile and hugged her. Later he told his new friends he didn't care if it was a boy or a girl. But his wife knew he preferred a boy.

Getting settled in a new city was both a hectic and exciting time. Between preparing for a new baby and the interstate move, there was little time to worry about other things. That would come later.

In a few months, Michael held his first child in his arms. He was thrilled that she was a girl. He gladly took turns rocking her to sleep and feeding her. He cheered her on when she took her first steps and said her first words. To Michael, his daughter was brighter and prettier than all other babies on the planet.

He quickly found a job working with juveniles and the couple set down roots in Texas. He continued to visit relatives in Mississippi, but he never returned to his hometown. When in Mississippi he would occasionally run into family members of former friends and ask about those he remembered fondly. As much as he wanted to visit his former home, he knew it wasn't possible. It would be too upsetting for all concerned. Texas was his home now, and it was home to his growing family. The following year, his wife gave birth to another girl. He laughed and said he was surrounded by females, with no males to even the score. He was happy with his new daughter but now wished for a boy he could give his name to.

He helped raise his little girls. Looking back to when he was seventeen, Michael could not have imagined being married, being the father of two happy babies, or even having a fulfilling job. He enjoyed his work and felt he had made the right decision by moving to Texas. He continued to maintain contact with his parents. Typewritten responses from his former attorney were highly prized. Those letters kept him informed of life in his hometown and the people he missed. He often thought of the former classmates he played football with. His former attorney was a lifeline of sorts for the young man.

He never stopped thinking of his grandmother, the one he killed. His guilt and regret were constant companions. He wished she were alive to spoil his daughters, and to share so many milestones in his life, including his college graduation, marriage, and law school. There were times he could almost remember what he had done to her, but not quite. The red mist never really lifted.

Michael continued to attend therapy sessions weekly. His medication had to be changed several times, due to side effects that developed. There were moments he wanted to ditch the pills he took on a regular basis. He felt as normal as anyone else. He suffered from no hallucinations, no voices, no delusions or paranoia. He felt well enough to get off medications. Whenever he expressed his wishes to discontinue the medications, his wife gave him a loud and firm no. He agreed to do as his therapist instructed but still wished that someday he could discontinue the medication. Part of him wanted desperately to be declared normal, to live a normal life, without any reminders of his past sickness, to finally leave the past in the past; that's what he wanted more than anything.

John Mason enjoyed the letters from his former client. They were full of hope and accomplishment. He counted his former client as one of his success stories. The fact that Michael was released from a hospital for the insane to attend college and to get a degree was amazing. Applying for law school, getting married, and becoming a father was nothing short of a miracle. He wished he could share his happiness with Michael, but the fact that many were still hurt by the murder and its aftermath weighed heavy on his mind.

John worried that Michael did not understand that things would never be normal for him. The shadow of his slain grandmother will always be present for those who remember that June day in 1957. During their first year in Texas, the young couple decided to split their Christmas trip between Vicksburg and Alabama. That way they could introduce both families to the new baby. It proved to be a happy time for all, except for Michael's father. Mike stayed drunk most of the holidays which was disturbing for the couple. During the last day of their visit, Michael confronted his father. While he and his wife were visiting relatives in Vicksburg, they sat in the living room looking at family pictures, when Mike staggered in. When he almost slipped on a floor rug and practically fell into a waiting chair, Michael yelled, "Daddy, you've had enough!"

"Don't tell me what to do. You're just like your mother," Mike, slurring the end of his words.

"Why do you drink? It ruins everything. Look what it did to me. And it ruined things between you and mama," exclaimed Michael, frustrated.

Unable to control his emotions, Michael continued to lambast his father. "My life was miserable growing up. I needed a father, but you weren't there for me. I swear I won't do that to my children" he yelled.

"Get out, get out!" screamed Mike.

Neither the father nor son ever reconciled their differences. The gap between them grew wider. The couple, however, did not want to give up on Mississippi. They were thinking of investing in real estate, perhaps buying land in the southeastern part of the State. Lauderdale County would be an area to explore. Somewhere far enough away from his former hometown and his drunken father.

CHAPTER TWENTY-SEVEN

(1971)

The years slipped past. Dramatic changes occurred on the national scene. The innocence of the early sixties gave way to assassinations and Watergate. Michael's desire to change the world, to leave his imprint on things, changed as well. Now it was a matter of getting each day's job done.

Michael's work with Texas juveniles grew increasingly difficult. The once easy communication between himself and the troubled youth was now strained. As the late 1960s passed into history and a new decade began, he grew weary. Drugs and the formation of gangs invaded every aspect of his work with juveniles. Every day, he came home sad and angry. His wife was concerned. Michael's visits to the therapist became less frequent and his medication began having negative side effects.

It was the couple's habit to sit outside, under a giant oak tree, and discuss the day's events. It was a hot day in late August. As they sipped iced tea, Janice urged, "You need to make an appointment with your therapist. You know it's long overdue."

"What do you mean long overdue?" he asked.

"You're depressed, frustrated, and in a sour mood most of the time. That's what I mean."

"I'm sorry," he apologized.

Janice continued, "I know you're miserable. You need to talk it out. And your medication, it needs changing."

He agreed to make an appointment the following day. The conclusion at his session with his doctor was that he needed a change in career. He laughed to himself. Michael knew that already. He didn't need a psychiatrist to tell him he needed a change. He thought longingly of Lauderdale County. The couple began to spend weekends in Mississippi, searching for land to buy. After six months, they found what they were looking for. Lush acres of land a number of miles outside of the town of Meridian. Michael man gave his notice at work, then he and Janice packed up the family's belongings and moved back to Mississippi.

Once again, Michael had to decide what he wanted to do next. Taking the bar and practicing law did not appeal to him. Neither did working with juveniles. His new medication didn't help. He was becoming increasingly depressed. What he needed was the serene atmosphere of nature; to be hidden away from town and the people in it.

Together the couple decided on land development. Janice got a teaching job at a local community college. Michael used the money he had saved and inherited from family members to buy land. A division of property grew from the purchased land. Also, new on the horizon was another baby. This time it was a boy. Michael gave his son his name.

He didn't care if some thought his name was infamous, forever connected with a gruesome murder. He was proud of his name and no amount of bloodletting could erase that fact. He lived far enough away from his hometown and many years had passed since the murder. It shouldn't matter what he named his son. It was Michael's grandfather's name. It was the name his father had given him. It was good enough for his son.

Michael adored his three children and took pride in everything they did. He was especially proud of his new son. When little Michael was old enough, he taught him to ride a bike and swim. He dreamed of watching his son play football, to be a running back. He imagined him on the baseball field. Little Mikey was handsome like his father. A bright boy, who grew up knowing nothing of his father's history. The children of the couple did not know of the murder or the subsequent trial. It was the stuff of nightmares. Their father didn't want to damage their childhoods with trauma. His upbringing had been forever tainted. The couple agreed there was no reason to burden their children with their father's tragic past. It was something they would not learn about for many years. It would be their mother's duty to one day share their father's dark secret with them.

In 1971, the young family found some measure of peace. The birth of their third child and new careers for the couple kept them busy. There was little time to worry about the past. But every now and then, Michael had a brief glimpse behind the red mist. It came during the night. When his dreams pierced the mist he woke up screaming, but he never remembered what caused it. In his mind, he knew it was his grandmother. It was her lasting gift to him. It didn't matter how he prayed for relief or how often he visited his therapist. The guilt and horror would never leave him. He even imagined what it would be like to have his grandmother in his young life. To have her die peacefully in her bed, surrounded by family. Whenever he imagined a different ending for her, his eyes filled with tears. He would sometimes have to go somewhere quiet, where he could sob freely.

As his children grew older, they began to notice their father's changing moods. Sometimes they would hear him crying in the bathroom. The running water couldn't hide his pain. They would ask their mother, "What's wrong with Daddy?"

She would answer with, "Nothing, little ones. Daddy's just sad because he can't change the bad things that happen in this world."

When they were little, that response would satisfy them.

All three children were very bright. Little Michael was especially good with numbers. He told his wife their children would be successful.

"I remember when I was in my cell, awaiting trial. I wrote to my English teacher. I told her I was destined for death, or a life full of fame and riches.

Maybe I was thinking of the little ones I would one day have. They are so bright, so hard working and studious."

Janice smiled. "I'm sure they will be successful. But it may not mean fame or riches. There are other ways to be successful, my love."

He sat back, nodding in agreement.

CHAPTER TWENTY-EIGHT

(1975)

Michael treasured the letters he received from his former attorney, John Mason, and kept them under lock and key in a roll-top desk in the couple's living room. It's where he put all his important papers. Like clockwork, he received a type-written letter from John once a month. In the most recent letter, good news was shared. The attorney's ten-year-old son won another tennis tournament. That son would grow to be 6'2", an exceptional tennis player who participated in numerous tournaments around the state. He would one day become an attorney himself. He was a favorite in the community, the previous hometown of the attorney's infamous former client. This and future letters included pictures of the beloved son.

The letters mentioned the marriage of his oldest daughter and the birth of a grandchild. His youngest daughter also went to law school and later practiced law with her father. John's son, who played football with Michael, received a degree in business administration. That son later worked in state government. The communications from John also included information about Michael's former classmates and their families.

Michael's father still drank himself to sleep every night. As a result, Michael kept his children away from Mike. He enjoyed sharing those same children with his mother, Lisa. It gave Lisa joy to see the man her son had become. She felt it was a miracle.

Like her son, Lisa had left her former hometown. She returned only for brief visits. She couldn't stand the curious looks, the long stares, or the embarrassing questions. She realized the town would not forget the murder until her son's generation had died out. After a time, she ended those visits altogether.

Michael's children continued to grow and earn their father's respect. He loved to brag about their numerous accomplishments. Janice also found her niche. She enjoyed her work at the local college. Janice formed lasting friendships with students and faculty members. She told her husband she never wanted to leave Lauderdale County. He agreed. He finally felt at home after such a long time. When he left for Whitfield, he believed he would never find a home again. In Lauderdale County, he found a local therapist he liked. They formed a bond that didn't exist with her former psychiatrists. He discussed his need to lift the mist. Michael wanted to live in the present and look forward to a future with his family. The therapist suggested hypnosis.

The first four sessions were extremely painful for him. They brought back his difficult childhood. Michael remembered in vivid detail the bloody abuse his mother suffered at the hands of the drunken husband. He remembered her fear and the terror in her eyes. It physically sickened him. The disgust he felt should have given him hope. It was an obvious result of his recovery. But it caused little comfort when he thought of how his mother had suffered.

Next came the nightmares. These he remembered with clarity. His doctor agreed to discontinue the hypnosis for the time being. His sessions consisted of talk therapy and another change in medication. Every few years, Michael either developed side effects from his medications or they ceased to be effective. This was frustrating for him since he didn't want to take the pills in the first place.

His therapist assured his patient that new medications were being developed almost daily to deal with various mental diseases, including schizophrenia. It gave Michael little comfort. It still tied him to his mental illness. He wondered if he would ever be free of its effects.

When his oldest child was seven, Michael drove her to dance class, mainly ballet. He attended her dance recitals. But it was her position as a pitcher on her softball team that brought out his fatherly pride. His second daughter, who at age six, was a budding writer. He encouraged her through nightly storytelling. She would entertain the family with tales of rabbits that talked and dogs that did the twist.

His four-year-old learned to count when he was three. Numbers was his thing. He was very athletic, just like his father, learning to ride a bike early on and to swim like a fish. Michael was already playing catch with his four-year-old.

His children were what kept him going. Most of the time he managed to dispel bouts of depression by involving himself in his children's pursuits. He also took to writing in a journal, at his therapist's suggestion. The doctor believed Michael's refusal to let go of the memory, along with the guilt of what he did, wouldn't go away unless he confronted it. The best way to do that was to examine it through his writing. He wrote quite a bit during those last months of 1975, and he turned the writings over to the psychiatrist for discussion and evaluation. He didn't understand his past rage and his destructive nature. He felt he was so different from the young man who was filled with such hate that he totally destroyed his former home. How could he mutilate his beloved grandmother? The hideousness of it wouldn't leave him alone.

"I don't understand why I did it" the man told his doctor.

"You were in the overt stage of schizophrenia which was aggravated by the consumption of alcohol, that's why."

"But I was a bully as a child. I did terrible things, but now I would choke any boy who did the same thing to one of my daughters."

"Unfortunately, you didn't receive the treatment you needed when you were young. So it manifested itself during your teen years. It came to a head during those summer months of 1957," explained the therapist.

Still confused, the man asked, "But why?"

"It was always there. Even as a child. It just grew and became more obvious, as you grew older. The alcohol didn't help."

"Could I have inherited it from my father?" Michael wondered.

"Possibly -- your father is very violent, is he not?"

"Yes."

"And he drinks a lot?"

"Yes, like me that day in June."

"Yes," said the doctor. "Exactly."

Michael leaned forward in his chair, his head in his hands.

"I wish I could let go of it all, the memory, the guilt, the sheer awfulness of it all. I want to be like other people," he cried out in anguish. During one of these sessions, Michael agreed to try hypnosis again.

CHAPTER TWENTY-NINE

(1977)

Michael's weekly sessions with his therapist helped up to a point. He was still young but edging quickly to middle age. As time passed, he felt his illness more acutely. His depression had deepened over time. The medication only worked with the assistance of other therapies that included hypnosis.

The children were older now. His daughters were ten and nine. His boy had turned six. The one bright light in his existence were his children. He couldn't help but wonder if he would live to watch his kids grow to maturity. He had a deepening fear that he wouldn't grow old like others of his generation. His wife wanted him to get extra treatment. She urged him to enter the hospital for examination and whatever therapy was needed. He refused but increased his sessions with his psychiatrist. Under hypnosis, he remembered more about his childhood but very little about that day in June 1957.

There were times when the red mist lifted briefly but stopped short of revealing the events of that day. Letters from John Mason came once a month. The lawyer's youngest daughter had recently married. His oldest had divorced and remarried and taught school for over twelve years, enlightening sixth graders on the history of Latin America. His oldest son continued to work for the State. His youngest son was involved in numerous school activities. Besides being a member of the band, Michael was on the tennis and golf team. His height gave a good indication that he would also play basketball.

John also gave Michael news of his former friends from his hometown. He told of marriages and births. The deaths of older citizens of his hometown were also included in the monthly letters. Michael continued to prize these communications, not so much for the news, but for the relationship he continued to have with his former counselor. His admiration and respect for him never ceased. He was grateful for the past legal representation he received. But more than that, he was happy for the hand of friendship the older man had given him when he was a troubled teenager. He appreciated their continued relationship.

The management of Michael's real estate business in Lauderdale County continued to occupy his time. Selling parcels of his purchased property to establish the subdivision bearing his family name was a labor of love. Janice continued to work for the local community college. She shared her experiences with her husband in hopes of cheering him up. She often organized family excursions to lighten her husband's mood. They took a trip to the Jackson Zoo. They also toured the old Capitol, the Governor's Mansion, and several antebellum mansions. It did give temporary relief. Next, she planned a camping trip to teach the children how to cook on an open fire and to set up a tent.

Being outdoors was a real treat, not only for her children but for Michael as well. Nature seemed to be uplifting for him. It made him happier than anything else. Janice decided to plan weekend trips to various sites throughout the state. Wherever they camped, Michael would rise early and take long walks. He usually ended up near a pond, stream or waterfall. It seemed to calm him. He laughed and said it was obvious he was descended from Vikings, due to his love of water.

When his father was in ill health, Michael found it necessary to spend more time in Vicksburg. A lifetime of alcohol abuse had taken its toll. It was clear his father didn't have many years left. When he thought of his parents and his difficult childhood it was with sympathy. As a father himself, he realized that mistakes are easily made, despite good intentions. He understood his father's drinking was a sign of illness. He felt sad for his mother and what she endured. He admired her courage, in spite of all the hardships she faced. Michael wished he had been kinder to the both of them.

More and more, he thought of his hometown and the friends he grew up with. He remembered the times he would race his bicycle up and down the hills of his home. When he watched his daughter play softball, he thought of the Little League team he was part of. The games he played in the park with other boys his age came back in full force. Sometimes these memories brought joy, other times sadness. There were bittersweet thoughts because they were part of the past, images of things long over, long forgotten by some.

Michael knew he would never be famous or rich. Although they were comfortable, he would never be able to give his wife and children the financial security he truly wanted for them.

On an early September afternoon, Michael sat under a magnolia tree in the back yard staring straight ahead when Janice approached him. "What are you thinking of?" she asked.

Startled, he jumped and turned toward her. "What did you say?"

"I asked, what are you thinking of?" she repeated. He looked up at her with a sad smile and answered her question.

"The past, I guess. Futile dreams of wealth."

The woman leaned over and kissed her husband on the cheek and said, "Honey, we don't need wealth. We are fine as we are."

He reached up and took her hands in his. "I wanted to leave you and the kids secure. I want my children to have a college education. I want you to be able to retire when you want to. I want this house paid for. You don't need a mortgage hanging over you."

A look of concern crossed the woman's face, "You sound like you're not going to be here to take care of all that."

"I may not be here."

Alarmed, Janice demanded an explanation, "Just what do you mean?" she cried. The color in her face drained.

The man looked down at his hands and mumbled, "I don't know. I don't believe I'll make it to old age. I was never meant to be old."

"Don't say things like that" she cried.

He took her in his arms and hugged his wife. She began to cry. He assured her that he wouldn't do anything to himself. But deep down inside he wasn't so sure. Both Michael and Janice would never forget that conversation in early September. The wife would often repeat her husband's words to others close to her.

CHAPTER THIRTY

(July 18, 1980)

It was a typical summer day in South Mississippi, hot and humid. It started the way it usually did. Janice cooked breakfast for Michael and their three children. Over orange juice, toast, and eggs, the family made plans for the day. The oldest girl had dance lessons. Swimming lessons were on the schedule for the two younger children. The wife had a faculty meeting at the local community college. Registration for classes was starting in mid-August. Michael was the only one with no concrete plans for the day.

Around noon, he left the family home for a long walk. He needed to find a good place to think. As he walked beside the neighborhood lake, he thought about the past. That hot June in 1957 came to mind. He went over the events of his trial and its aftermath. The years spent at Whitfield came rushing back. He thought of his wife and children. The early years spent with his parents invaded his thoughts.

Michael's father had recently died of the effects of alcoholism. Years and years of abuse had taken its toll. It broke his heart to watch his father drink himself to death. Michael was grief-stricken over his father's demise. His mother, though relatively young, was also suffering from ill health. The strains of so much turmoil throughout her life affected her physically. Michael wondered if there was a curse on his family. What about his own children, he asked himself. Would his continued existence bring the curse into their lives? The violence and blood of those years caused renewed anguish.

But what hurt the most was what he did to his grandmother. He remembered her battered body lying on the floor in the hallway. He wondered what the homeplace looked like now. He had heard it hadn't been occupied since that day in June so many years ago. He even heard the place was haunted. That former home and what occurred in it certainly haunted him. In his mind's eye, he could see the overturned refrigerator, the smashed furniture, the broken China, the shattered glass, and the bloody tracks in each room. He saw himself dragging his grandmother from room to room - the red mist lifting briefly to show that grisly scene. Normally when he had these memories he would call his therapist and make an emergency appointment. But not this time.

He turned and headed back to the house. He entered his study and lifted the roll-top desk. He found his pistol and loaded it with bullets. Leaving the study, he went to his quiet place. The good no longer outweighed the bad. The red mist finally lifted as he raised his gun. He thought of leaving a note, but why bother? Let them wonder, he thought.

Tears glistened on his face. He pointed the gun and pulled the trigger. Blood gushed from his body as his brain shut down. No more thoughts. No more anguish. No more blame existed.

Later his family found the body. Janice remembered her husband's prediction that he would never grow old. There were tears, lots of them, and just as many questions that went unanswered. The days and weeks that followed were filled with funeral arrangements, estate matters, and picking out a lot at a nearby cemetery. What type of headstone to place at the burial site had to be decided. And finally, a decision about what to put on the headstone to sum up the life of the tortured man.

For months there was regret and unrelenting grief. People shook their heads and said, "what a waste." But those close to him didn't feel his life was a waste. There were the juveniles he helped, and the three children he helped bring into the world and raise. There was the love he shared with his wife, the girl from Alabama.

Michael had helped a number of teenagers who were afflicted with drug addictions. The man counseled them, got them help, and continued to support them through rehabilitation. Some had served time. He supported numerous young people through their incarceration and later, release. Many of those he helped went on to have successful lives.

His own children benefitted from the short time they had with their father. They had the lessons he taught them and many memories of dance recitals, baseball games, campouts, and holiday celebrations. He taught them so much – how to set up a tent, how to start a fire, and he taught his oldest how to drive. His children shared memories of dressing up for Halloween and going trick-or-treating with their father. They missed him on Thanksgiving and Christmas.   Despite all the good things, the shortness of time with their father, and the way he left the world, did its damage to the children. There was a pain that stayed with each child well into adulthood. The nightmares that caused the children to wake up screaming for the father persisted. The family needed counseling to deal with the trauma of Michael's bloody death.

John Mason received a letter from his wife family telling him of his client's suicide. He didn't share his sadness with his own family, but he did tell them about the man's death. There were many questions about his former client that he briefly answered then quickly changed the subject. It was obvious to his younger daughter that he was affected by his client's death, but he didn't share what he was feeling.

The story of the young man and what happened to him persisted in the mind of the lawyer's daughter. She never forgot the story. Southern Gothic, she called it. Later, much later, she wanted to share it with others.

After putting pen to paper, she had one last thing to do. She and a friend wanted to visit the murder house. They took Highway 49 and turned onto 433. After driving at least twenty minutes, they took a left onto Highway 3. The daughter and her friend ended up on a dirt road. On either side of the road were corn fields stretching as far as the eye could see. As they continued down the bumpy, uneven road, it became obvious there was no wooden Colonial-style home in the distance. As the dirt road began to even out, the two women saw a black truck coming toward them. They slowed down to let the truck pass. The women pulled over and her friend lowered the driver's side window. She asked the middle-aged driver about the location of the murder house. The man said he didn't know where it was, but he had a friend who did, and he phoned the friend to get directions. The women showed the man a picture of the house they believed to be the murder house. He looked at the photograph and exclaimed, "Those are my steps. That's my house that we recently purchased and renovated!"

The house in the photograph wasn't the murder house, but the man's house nearby that was recently renovated. The house was down the road from the murder house, probably built around the same time, maybe even by the same builder.

The man's house, when he bought it, was what is commonly referred to as a "fixer upper." He showed the women a picture of the recently renovated home. It was beautiful enough to be on an episode of HGTV. He said the home was over a hundred years old. The patio was paved with old bricks he had collected himself from an old building in Vicksburg. He finished his story by telling the women, "My wife thought I was crazy and wanted no part of my hairbrained project. I eventually convinced her of its potential and now she loves our home." He offered to show the women the home after they located and viewed the site of the original murder house.

They soon learned the ten-room Colonial-style home that once housed the grandmother and her 17-year-old grandson no longer existed. All that was left was a green field, surrounded by tall trees. No one knew if the house was torn down or was destroyed by fire. Nothing remained of what took place there so long ago. It was as if the house never existed. The general store that the Negro cook ran to was still there, although it had a fresh coat of white paint. It looked like a storage barn, not the country store it was in 1957.

The family that once played an important role in the small farming community, who lived in the county for generations, had long since moved away. Even the grandmother's three children had either died or lived elsewhere. The only evidence that the grandson had once lived in the county along with his aunts, cousins, and parents and stayed with his grandmother existed in the local library and newspaper archives.

The memory existed in the minds of those who played ball with Michael and went to school with him. But they were older now. The lawyer's daughter wondered who would remember once they were gone. She took a photograph of the empty field and drove away. It was an unsatisfactory ending to a story without closure.

EPILOGUE

Dear readers, what you just read is a fictionalized account of a true story. I am the youngest daughter of the attorney who represented the seventeen-year-old boy responsible for the death of his grandmother. I was nine years old when she was murdered, and when the subsequent trial took place.

As a child, I knew a little, but not much, about the facts of the case. Later, as a young woman, I learned more. Before I could discover most of what took place in 1957 and the following years, the man I called my father, the man who raised me and took me to Christmas parades and taught me to drive, passed away in 2003. Recently, I ran across a great deal of information about the seventeen-year-old and his murder trial. It was then that I decided to share the information with others through this book.

A large portion of what I discovered was memorialized in copies of *The Yazoo Herald* and in Ricks Memorial Library. I would also like to thank those who knew the boy and shared what they knew. For privacy's sake, their names have been changed. Nor will I share the boy's name or those of his immediate family. It is right that they should live their lives in tranquility and without judgment.

In researching and writing this novel, I discovered a great deal. I already knew about the trial process, as I am a criminal defense attorney. I enjoyed sharing criminal procedure, which included picking a jury, with my readers. In studying the treatment of the mentally ill, I was surprised to learn that Mississippi's State Hospital at Whitfield had a rich and varied history. I also discovered that in 1957, it was a self-contained facility with much to offer its patients.

Still, there were many questions left unanswered. To a limited degree, I found it necessary to fill in the blanks with fiction, although I tried to make the fiction as close to reality as possible. It was based upon what I already knew, and what I believed the characters in the book were likely to do. The murder and subsequent trial were based on the truth. Much of my description of the boy's stay at Whitfield is based on extensive research.

A great deal has changed since 1957, but there is one fact that remains the same. The diagnosis and treatment of the mentally ill, especially among the very young, is woefully inadequate. In the late 1950s, as in the present time, children who suffer mental illness often go undiagnosed, despite overt signs of psychological distress. People close to those children, including family members, teachers and other caregivers, sometimes ignore those signs. That can leave feelings of abandonment and depression. As the child grows into adulthood, those feelings can increase and lead to tragedy for all concerned.

In my work, I've seen this happen. Children who suffer become confused and angry juveniles. If there is a lesson to be learned from this sad story it is that we must take care of our youth. We shouldn't overlook and ignore our children. Every child needs a safe, loving place to grow. If there's trauma, get them the help they need. If they act violently, again get them the help they need, the earlier the better.

I am not a mental health professional, but I hope my cautionary tale will cause individuals to realize children need a safe and healthy environment. This is sorely needed in our troubled times.

www.ingramcontent.com/pod-product-compliance
Lightning Source LLC
Chambersburg PA
CBHW020043310726
48970CB00007B/2391